To Pat on your Birthday!

STOLEN DAISY

A NOVEL

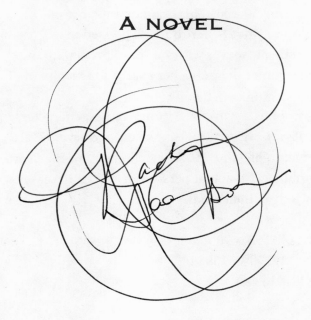

RACHAEL ISAACSON

ISBN: 0615952690
ISBN-13: 978-0615952697
Dirt Road Press

Cover Design © 2014 Rachael Isaacson
Author Photo © 2014 Amanda Carolan

Printed in the USA
First Edition

DEDICATION

To my husband, for believing in my talent from the moment I started my journey as a novelist. Thank you for your unwavering confidence in my ability, for acknowledging my passion for creativity and for all the nights you took care of our family as I worked into the early morning hours. I love you, always.

ACKNOWLEDGMENTS

To my three beautiful children—too young to fully understand what 'I have to work tonight' really means. You have been my motivation, so that you, too, will trust in your God given talents and follow the authenticity of your dreams.

Carolyn, Melissa and Tamara—thank you for taking the time to read 'Stolen Daisy' during my creative process. Thank you, too, for your candid feedback, suggestions and, above all, bringing the characters to life as they were read for the first time.

Tiffany—your love for the written word and your knowledge of the English language is inspiring. The time you spent with me in the beginning of the manuscript gave me the foundation, and the courage, to complete this story. You made me a better writer, and for that I am forever grateful. Thank you.

Amanda—my sister and best friend. Thank you for listening to me read, chapter-by-chapter, when the urge to share my newly created world was too much to hold in. You think I have all the answers, but the truth is you teach me more than you know. Thank you for the inspiration and love.

My parents—you both gave me a unique composition of rigid responsibility, compassion, and a yearning for creativity in my soul. The best of both of you. **And Becky**, my first little one. I cherish you and will always thank God for answering my prayers for another little sister, no matter what.

Andy—you are the definition of success. Not only because of all you have accomplished, but because you believed in yourself, knew what you were capable of, and had the courage to follow your calling. I am proud to call you brother (forget the in-law)—honored actually. You made this possible, after all, with your generosity (read: new mac book pro). Is sugar-brother a thing? Kidding.

The Isaacsons—all of you. From the moment I married into the family I have been inspired—and in awe of the success, love, laughter, and genuine goodness the entire family shares in common. All of you have inspired me strive for greatness, too. I am an Isaacson, after all.

Uncle Randy—Thank you for—without hesitation—offering your time, expertise, and advice. Your encouraging words helped propel me forward toward the finish line. I will always remember your kindness.

PROLOGUE

"**S**top right there, Arlene. Don't you dare follow me, you hear?"

The screen door slammed behind Chad, just as a violent clap of thunder echoed a warning across the sky. Arlene obeyed, which was against her nature. She needed to buy some time, so she paused, calculating how to keep Chad from driving off to the police.

"Chad please, come inside and talk to me, let me explain," Arlene offered sweetly. "Five minutes—that's all I'm asking." Chad stopped, but kept his backed turned to his pregnant wife.

"Five minutes—then do as you please. I'll let you go, you won't hear from me again. Of course, that means you'll never see this girl of ours either," Arlene continued. She rubbed her swollen belly, lowering her head to hide a smirk.

She had him, or so she thought. Manipulating Chad had always required less effort than any man she had controlled in her past. He was also the only man she had ever genuinely loved, as much as Arlene could love anyone, that is. And while most women would have been overjoyed with the partnership of such a devoted father, Arlene could not see past her own jealousy. Instead of nourishing the love for her family, her hatred grew. Arlene chose instead to feed her ravenous rage, until the dark shadows of her fury bled black throughout her soul.

All she saw before her now was a weak man who loved their first daughter, Jennifer, more completely in the very second she was born than he had ever loved his own wife. In Arlene's demented mind, such a man did not deserve his daughter's love in return.

Chad turned and walked closer to Arlene as the thunder growled above. Once close enough, he cradled Arlene's belly between his sturdy hands. He didn't want to touch Arlene, but he had to connect with his innocent baby who didn't deserve to grow in a womb full of hate.

Lightning struck the ground behind their little shack and lit up Chad's face through the pouring rain, and in that flash, Arlene saw Chad's deep blue eyes piercing into her own, hard as stone. He backed away, dropped his hands to his sides. His once handsome, chiseled face now looked as worn and vacant as the wooden foundation of their secluded home, and his hair and beard were as unkempt as the wild weeds which grew tall above the metal awning of their rotting porch.

"Not this time, Arlene. Your games with me are over."

"Nothing's over, Chad, and you know it," Arlene said matter-of-factly. Babies need their mama's, which is why you'll stay with me. Forever."

"Just like Jennifer needed you?" Chad shouted. He knew better than to threaten Arlene, she proved to him what she was capable of, but his boiling rage took away his self-control. He spit his words into Arlene's face. "I will tell you just what is going to happen. You will have this baby in prison, and my little girl will come home with me—to a home you will never find. And you will return to your cold cell, and look out through the black bars of your cage for the rest of your goddamned life."

Arlene looked back at Chad in shock, and felt a twinge of panic as Chad turned and walked toward his truck. She had to do something to regain his attention, had to teach him a lesson for good. She let out a bellowing wail as she clutched her arms around her stomach, falling to her knees on the drenched gravel that led up to their home. As Chad rushed back to her, she quickly scraped her knees back and forth against the pebbled walk until she was sure that they bled, to solidify her attempt at stalling him as both urgent and believable.

It worked.

"Get up," said Chad, as he walked behind Arlene and hoisted her up from beneath her arms. "Sit down on the steps while I get something to clean you up." He returned with a washcloth, but the beating rain had already washed the blood from her knees and pooled into a diluted red bath beneath her bare, swollen feet.

"Is the baby okay?" asked Chad, his voice filled with concern as he tended her wounds, repulsed by her exposed and soiled skin.

"Of course she's all you care about. Never mind your wife," replied Arlene, through her manufactured sobs. The rain streamed down her face and hair and hid the complete absence of any authentic tears from her emotionless eyes.

But Arlene's cries no longer worked. Her years of toying with his heart, using his devotion to his child against him, made Chad almost as hard as Arlene herself. "Get inside, Arlene. Lie down and put your feet up, I'm sorry I caused you stress, that's the last thing the baby—you and the baby need right now."

He had to get away from her, needed to get to the police station with the evidence before it was too late. "I just need to go blow off some steam, Ar. You're right, as always. You do know me. And I can't leave you, just like I can't leave our new baby. Go lie down and rest, I'll pick up another bag of ice to chew. You've got to keep cool in this heat."

Fucking liar, thought Arlene as she smiled sweetly up at him. "I knew you would come around and do what is best for our family," she said as she raised herself off the porch steps and climbed toward the house. Before opening the screen door, she turned and called out to Chad. "Can I give you something first?"

"When I get back," he said as he pulled the key out of the lock and opened the door to his pickup.

"No. Now."

"Whatever it is, it can wait 'till I get back..." Chad hesitated, worried that Arlene would call his bluff and disappear before he could make things right.

"It's a card. From Jennifer. She drew it for your birthday, just before she went missing."

Arlene saw him break, watched his face soften at the moment she said their daughter's name.

"She couldn't wait for you to see it—she learned to write 'DAD' all by herself, can you believe it? Come back to the porch and out of the rain already," she said as she walked into the house.

Chad knew he should get into his truck and peel away, but the ache in his heart for his sweet Jennifer, the chance to hold a last desperate connection with her, clouded his better judgment.

He slammed the rusted red door to his old Chevy and walked slowly back to the porch, his heart pounding like a bass drum in his tightening chest.

He stood on the porch, his back to the door, and watched the storm beat relentlessly into the muddy ground. Wind whipped through the mighty oak tree that towered over the house, tossing the massive branches back and forth effortlessly, while the tree's thick trunk stood strong against the assault.

This will all be over soon, Chad thought, as he struggled to keep his own storm of emotions in check. Thunder boomed above once more, silencing the creak of the screen door as Arlene quietly returned.

"Turn around, Chad."

Chad turned and locked into Arlene's sinister glare, her scowling face sharp with lines of icy rage. She looked wild as her eyes moved rapidly from side to side, with pupils fully dilated over her irises of honey green. Arlene's eyes appeared pure black, reflecting her deadly intentions. Chad shivered.

"I've waited patiently for you to understand we will always be together," Arlene began. "I will always be your only family. I will always be number one—with or without Jennifer."

Before Chad could respond, Arlene removed her hands from behind her back, revealing a Smith & Wesson revolver. She pointed the five-inch barrel directly at his heart. Chad began to speak but was silenced by the click of the disarmed safety.

"I always win, don't I?" Arlene said. "This could have been avoided, Chad. This is *your* fault. Am I so hard to love? Haven't I given you everything? Haven't I forgiven you over and over, forgiven you each time you tried to leave me? Forgiven you for that whore all those years ago?"

Arlene paused for a moment to savor the satisfaction of Chad's horror-stricken face.

"You didn't think I knew about that, did you? Imagine her surprise when she opened her front door and found me standing on her porch. Somebody had to tell her about us, had to make her realize she meant nothing to you and never would. I always took care of you, don't you see? But now here you are, stupid as always, trying to leave me again. Trying to get rid of me forever."

"Arlene, stop. You have things all wrong—

"Shut-up" Arlene screamed. "You've left me no other choice, don't you see? I ALWAYS WIN."

And with that, Arlene fired a single round into Chad's chest. The bullet shredded through his lung and began a deadly path through the center of his heart, exiting his back only after tearing through each layer of muscle and flesh in between. Arlene stood steady, as smoke billowed around the barrel of her gun, and watched with satisfaction as Chad fell lifelessly down the porch steps. He landed flat on his back against the muddy gravel, his eyes frozen open in death as the rain pummeled into his vacant stare. His arms landed outstretched on each side of his body in complete symmetry, which seemed to expel his soul into heaven like the pure majesty of a soaring dove.

Arlene, merciless in her need for revenge, hovered in front of Chad's body, aimed the gun toward his groin, and fired shot after shot between his legs until there was nothing more to offer than the silent click of an empty gun.

CHAPTER ONE

Samantha Beckett woke up, tangled in a sweaty mix of sheets and stuffed animals, a pair of chubby legs sprawled over her own. She opened her eyes and looked over at a sweet sleeping face covered in dirt, with strawberry blond ringlets stuck to rose-colored cheeks and long black eyelashes that curled up in perfection above her peacefully closed eyes. She smiled as she stroked back Daisy's curls and her heart swelled with love. Her little sister, Daisy, had made her way into Samantha's bed sometime in the middle of the night. Again.

Sam wished she could stay in bed with her sweet three-year-old girl all morning long, but it was Monday, and the start of another excruciatingly long school week. Skipping school was no longer an option for her. Once their mother, Beth Beckett, began sharing the outlet of her rage with Daisy too, Sam tried to be home every second possible in order to deflect Daisy's mistakes onto herself. She had called the attendance hotline and pretended to be her mother in order to stay home and protect her Daisy as often as she could. Sam was used to her mother's blows, and thought she deserved them most of the time, unlike Daisy, who just didn't know any better.

At the end of the fall semester Beth had received a call from Sam's homeroom teacher, who had grown concerned with her truancy record and failing grades. Up until then, on days that her mother failed to get out of bed to go to work or came home early, Sam explained away her presence by telling her mother there was no school that day, or that she had been sent home by the school nurse because of her chronic headaches. She did indeed have headaches, but Sam rarely complained of them out loud, as to do so would warrant a punch to the back of her head from her mother for, 'making shit up'. Sam had learned quickly that her only option was to suffer them in pain splitting silence.

The day her mother received the phone call which exposed her deceit, Sam received the worst beating of her 12-year-old life. Normally,

Beth would channel her angry punches into the areas of Sam's body where clothing would keep the blue and purple remnants of her fury cloaked in secrecy. This day, however, was much different.

Beth explained to Sam's teacher that her absence record was due to her severe migraines, and thanked her sincerely for looking out for her daughter. She went on to explain that Sam would not be in school for the rest of the week, as they were traveling out-of-state to a new doctor, one that specialized in adolescent neurology. Beth spun the perfect story of how her dear Samantha was to undergo a battery of tests that, she was sure, would find the cause of her constant pain once and for all.

Sam sat as still as hiding prey, as the lies slide effortlessly from her mother's mouth. Her surroundings became out of focus and her mother's voice faded slowly from her ears, as if Sam were sinking deep beneath the waters surface, fighting to remain conscience under the unforgiving pressure surrounding her head. Sam knew exactly why her mother had calculated that excuse to keep her out of school for so long, and she was about to endure the punishment that disgusting children like her deserved. Nobody embarrassed Beth Beckett, especially not her children whom she regarded as nothing more than worthless burdens.

Now that leaving Daisy was the only option, Sam began teaching her how to be a good girl, and how to stay out of their mother's way; and she prayed every day that her efforts would be enough to keep Daisy safe.

Sam picked up Daisy's favorite doll, a peculiar looking homemade doll with a plush body crocheted together with orange yarn. The dolls plastic face promised to be forever happy with its big blue eyes, and cherry red lips that smiled with the happy glee of a nurtured baby. She sweetly kissed Daisy's cheek, put the doll in her arms, and snuck out of bed. Leaving was easier, much easier, when she just snuck away.

Sam gathered her clothes and crept to the bathroom to get dressed. She put on jeans that were paper thin with wear and an inch too short. Her turquoise shirt, which used to be her favorite, had a large pink flower sewn to the seam where her sleeve and scooped collar met, and accented her neck and pretty collarbone, the one feature she sort-of admired. But now the shirt was just a little too tight which showed the world her changing body, especially her growing chest. She looked at her reflection in the mirror, blurred from her old plastic glasses and their outgrown prescription, and saw the fire of embarrassment rise in her cheeks.

No wonder nobody loves me. I'm a disaster just like mom says, Sam thought. She brushed her teeth with the remaining bristles left on her old toothbrush, combed her curly brown hair, and wished that she had a bobby pin to keep her unruly bangs out of the way.

What Sam could not see, however, was how her hair had the texture and body, with natural curls, that women spent hours trying to emulate. The color, which rose in her cheeks, coupled with the turquoise of her shirt, made her blue eyes sparkle with depth and radiance. Yes, Sam was beautiful. But no one had ever told her so.

Then, as always, Sam set out Daisy's breakfast, filled her cup with juice, and checked in on their mother to make sure she had made it home safely. The night before, Beth had another date with another new man, and trouble always seemed to follow her no matter how hard she tried to find a 'good one'. She was there, still dressed in her mini skirt and black nylon stockings, her makeup still intact. Samantha estimated their mother hadn't been in bed for long. Quietly, Sam tiptoed through the living room to the front door, and closed it silently behind her as she mentally prepared for the day ahead.

As soon as Sam headed down the porch steps, she caught a glimpse of Amy and Eileen walking up the sidewalk, looking perfect as usual in their fresh white capris and blue jean jackets. Sam thought it was ridiculous how the girls always coordinated their outfits to match. In fact, many of the 8th grade girls dressed the way Amy told them to as a way to uphold their place in the delicate and ever-complicated social circle of a pre-teen girl.

The girls walked toward Sam with their hair perfectly in place, Amy's shiny brown curls bobbing up and down over her shoulders, held back with a pink headband, and Eileen's blond bob tucked cutely behind her ears which highlighted her beautiful jawline and pink gloss covered lips.

Samantha sighed, "*damn-it.*"

"Oh look, it's Smelly Samantha, no time for a bath again this week, I see," Amy hissed out.

That was true, Samantha didn't bathe often. Their water service had been shut off for months, and even now with the water back on, shampoo and soap were luxury items that were often hard to come by. Sam had been stealing soap from the bathrooms at school by pumping as much of the pink liquid as possible into a zip-lock bag to keep herself and Daisy clean. That had worked for a while, until the day Amy walked in and caught her; and then spread the story of her humiliation to the entire 8th grade class.

Even though every cell in Sam's body screamed to run back into the dark shield her house provided, she forced her legs forward, step by step. She kept her head down and glimpsed up, only for a moment, through her long bangs, which had already fallen out of place and into her eyes. Amy's smug smile made her stomach churn. Why am I so worthless, Sam chanted in her head, along with all of her usual self-deprecating thoughts. She walked down the last few steps unnaturally slow to ensure that her walk to school would be at a comfortable distance behind her classmates. Just as Sam found the courage to glance up once more, she saw Eileen looking back at her, for just a brief moment.

At first, she mistook Eileen's expression as pity and sadness. But as Sam walked ahead, and processed the warmth she had felt from the girl's eyes, it was clear to her that Eileen was looking at her with a strange combination of understanding and regret.

What could Eileen possibly understand about my life, Sam thought.

CHAPTER 2

Daisy woke up with an enormous yawn and blinked her big eyes until the line between her dream and reality was less blurred. She felt the emptiness of the room and remembered that Samantha had school that day. She didn't understand why her Sammy had to leave her so often, and she did not like it one bit. She clutched her doll, crawled out of bed and tiptoed to the bathroom.

She did not dare flush.

Even at three years old, Daisy would rather be alone in the silent house than wake her mother and suffer the consequences of Beth's interrupted sleep.

She sat down at the table to eat. Samantha did the hard part by putting the milk in the bowl before she left, but Daisy could never seem to pour the cereal without making a mess. She tried and she tried, but she was never careful enough.

"You clumsy ass," her mother would say.

After scooping up the colorful fruit rings that had spilled around her bowl, Daisy ate her breakfast as quietly as she could as she looked out the cracked kitchen window. At least the sun is out, she thought cheerfully to herself. The long days seemed less scary to Daisy when the sun was out. The bright light, which beamed through the dusty window, brought life into the dark kitchen; a false cheer upon dingy walls that were once yellow, not that Daisy ever knew her house painted that happy color. She she sang her favorite song in her head as her legs dangled happily off of the cold metal chair.

Oh I was born, in the bright, bright morn'
when the sky was brilliant blue!
My mommy smiled, and cried, and styled—
my clothes just ever-so!
She hugged and sniffed,
and kissed my lips—
I was her pride and joy!

Just as her legs began to swing in rhythm with her melody, she heard her mother's bed squeak. Daisy inhaled sharply, and then held her breath. She quickly hopped off of her chair, took her bowl to the sink, and tried to find a place to put it among the overflowing dishes occupying all available space. She had only seconds...she gingerly placed it on top of the dirty pile, closed her eyes, and braced for the disastrous crash of the tower as it fell to the floor. Silence. She opened her eyes, saw the bowl had obeyed her placement, and smiled a proud smile. She tiptoed back to the old grey graphite table, grabbed the box of cereal, and dashed away to her hiding spot. Today she would have something to eat while she waited for her mother to leave for work. She smiled again. I sure am getting smart, she thought.

CHAPTER 3

Samantha arrived at school just in time to run to the bathroom. Just the sight of her school, so big and ominous with its dark brick walls and immense levels of grey windows, made Sam sick to her stomach with nervous anxiety. The school looked ancient with layers of thick ivy that scaled all the way to the rooftop, which to most enhanced the historical beauty of the institution. But to Sam, the ivy simply trapped the brick beneath its merciless grip and slowly suffocated the building, just as the building suffocated her.

She pushed open the bathroom door to absolute emptiness and was flooded with relief. Just the sight of the empty space gave her time to calm her nerves and clean up a bit before heading to her classroom. She splashed water on her face hoping to cool the rose colored heat from her cheeks, smoothed her unruly brown hair, and headed out to face the unavoidable viciousness ahead; a lions den cloaked in the docile disguise of a picture-perfect junior high classroom.

"Good Morning, Class!" said Sam's homeroom teacher, Ms. Chandler. "I trust you all had a wonderful weekend. Who would like to share something fun or noteworthy that happened?"

Josh Thompson's hand shot straight up and Sam could feel his excited energy radiating next to her.

"On Saturday afternoon I had a baseball scrimmage and hit three home-runs in the first inning. Coach took me to lunch because I dominate my team. I'm gonna to lead us to first place this year."

"Of course the coach said you dominate your team," said Amy. "He's your *Dad*."

The class chuckled at her wit.

"Whatever, Amy. Don't be so jealous," Josh replied with a confident grin. "I *am* that good."

"Well good for you Josh," said Ms. Chandler. "There is no better feeling than finding a passion, and putting in the hard work that your success demands."

"Who else would like to share?"

Olivia raised her hand.

"I had a sleepover on Saturday night with all of my best friends. It was super fun, and we stayed up all night laughing and playing games. Amy cut my bangs and everyone agreed I look much better with bangs." Olivia and Amy nodded at each other, and smirked in joint agreement.

"Samantha, would you like to share something special about your weekend?" asked Ms. Chandler.

Oh my god, why is Ms. Chandler always doing this to me, Sam screamed in her head. All of her other teachers treated Sam the way everybody did—like she was invisible. Sam could not understand why Ms. Chandler would not do the same.

"Sam didn't do anything over the weekend. She stayed home in her dirty old house like she always does," Amy spit out.

"That is quite enough. All of you, take out your first period assignment or use this time to finish any incomplete homework. Amy, see me after class."

Samantha almost wished she felt embarrassed, but more and more often, she just felt plain numb. And empty. And unworthy of the happiness her classmates came about so easily.

She was embarrassed of her house and how it contrasted against the rows of manicured homes in her middle class neighborhood, with its neglected lawn and missing pieces of siding from last year's big storm. Her dilapidated home was just one more confirmation to Sam that she was poor trash amongst her shiny peers.

Finally, the bell rang through the classroom, and as quickly as possible Sam picked up her books, kept her head down and ran out of the room. If she didn't exit with absolute haste, Ms. Chandler would give her that look of pity, or worse, try to stop her to talk. Sam knew her teacher meant well, but she could not look someone so beautiful in the eyes. Ms. Chandler's eyes were a soft shade of baby blue, which deepened underneath the warmth of her compassion. She kept her soft blonde curls pinned perfectly around her head, which glistened, even under the unflattering fluorescent classroom lights. Sam thought herself unworthy of this woman's attention and her brain would never form the right words to say, forcing her to stand frozen in silence as her mind raced and tripped over it's own thoughts. She always left their conversations feeling as dumb as she most certainly must have looked.

Sam was losing the battle against her depression and, if not for Daisy, she would have ended her pain in the only way she thought possible, long ago. She fought every day to make it through to the next, as she did not have the luxury of selfishness. She was her sister's only hope.

CHAPTER 4

Daisy! Where the hell are you! You have a big mess to clean up, stupid girl. How many goddamn times do I have to tell you not to leave your juice out! I knocked it over and now my morning is *screwed* because you had pissed me off—is it too much to ask I sit down at my own *goddamn* kitchen table and drink my coffee without having to look at your shit everywhere!" screamed Beth, at the top of her lungs.

Of course Beth did not spill the juice on accident. She smacked the cup off the table in a fit of anger as she looked at her phone and read a text from the man she had gone out with the night before. He apologized and said he was heading out of town for work and could not take her out that evening as he had promised. Sure,

Beth thought as her temper bloomed, "heading out of town." She needed to start controlling her desires and start playing a little harder to get if she were going to find the next man to support her insatiable appetite for beautiful things. One that will finally support her the way she deserves. A man with enough money to end her misery, and ensure she will never have to work another day of her life. Thoughts like these ran constant in Beth's head and controlled her every calculated action.

Her temper subsided as she shook her head and thought that he was too fat to put up with anyway. "No more cheap whiskey for me," she said to herself in the empty kitchen, as she stared at her phone. "The only thing I get in return is full between the legs and empty in the head," she laughed, as she vowed to make much better choices in her liquor and her men.

Meanwhile, Daisy tucked herself into a ball in the corner of her closet to hide from her mother's tantrum. She piled dirty clothes on top of herself to completely conceal her whereabouts as she trembled with worry that her mother would to care enough to come looking this time. She kept as still and quiet as she could manage, just like Sammy had taught her to do.

"I'm not kidding girl! I don't have time to clean up after dirty-ass brats like I'm some sort of slave around here. I work hard enough as it is" Beth shouted on her way out the door.

Then Daisy heard the front door slam and sighed with relief. She crawled out from her bunker with her box of cereal and skipped to the couch to wait for Sam, hoping that she would be home soon. It wasn't long before Daisy became restless with waiting though, so she went looking for something that would make her big sister smile. Once she found what she was looking for, Daisy covered her mouth to muffle the sweet giggle that escaped her throat, and jumped all the way down the hall with excitement. Her eager anticipation of how happy her Sammy would be when she got home kept her body tingling with excitement for the rest of the afternoon.

CHAPTER 5

The final bell rang and ended Sam's misery. Today was a success, all things considered. Other than the episode in homeroom everybody had let her be. Nobody tried to trip her in the hallway, nobody ridiculed her at lunch, and no other teachers tried to get her to participate in class discussions. All in all a good day, and, the best part was, the week was already halfway over.

She headed home to rescue Daisy and start preparing her dinner. Daisy always waited for Sam to get home from school in her usual spot, curled up like a little kitten on the back of the living room couch, staring out patiently from behind the grime covered front window. Sam rounded the corner and felt relief to see her sweet baby waiting there as always, shining her happiness out for all to see. Daisy's innocent beauty radiated from her big blue eyes and cherub cheeks, despite her dirty clothes and tangled hair.

"Hi baby girl! I missed you so much!"

"Sammy!" Daisy cried out. "Guess what! I found your special book in mommy's room!"

"Oh, honey" sighed Sam. "You know what mom will do if she catches you in her room." But she smiled and hugged Daisy. "Thank you so much, sunshine."

Samantha's special book is one bound with leather and filled with blank ledger paper. She had found it in the attic of the house last year when one Saturday afternoon, during Daisy's nap, Sam had finally summoned the courage to investigate the mysterious door that hid invitingly in the ceiling of her bedroom closet.

She found the book right away looking lonely and discarded amongst the dust and boxes. Boxes that, for reasons Sam couldn't understand, gave her a feeling of terror. She grabbed the book and climbed down from the cramped space with a careful quickness. She wiped off the dust with the bottom of her shirt, thumbed through the pages— their edges beautifully coated in gold—and inhaled the musty odor as she closed her eyes. She knew just what she would do with her new treasure.

She began filling the pages with her stories, daydreams really, that filled her heart with longing, with jealousy, and with a strange sense of hope. Sam's writing soon became Daisy's bedtime stories as she fell asleep to a different world weaved together with beautiful places and loving people.

That all ended the night their mother stormed into the room and snatched the book off of the bed, just as Sam tossed it from her hands as if she was caught with an illicit possession. Such a thing was forbidden as happiness was not tolerated in their home, and the more Daisy's love for Samantha grew, the more their mother became enraged with uncontrolled disgust.

"Who do you think you are?" Sam's mother spat out. "Who'd you steal this book from?"

"I didn't steal it."

"You lying bitch. Tell me where you got this book." Her mother said again.

"I found it in the attic..."

As soon as Samantha uttered those words her mother's arm raised up, as Sam winced back in preparation. Beth's hand landed hard across Sam's face creating an echoed whack against tender flesh, and left a hate-filled handprint welted on Sam's cheek. A welt that reminded Sam that she was not loved. As if she really needed reminding.

Daisy crawled up into Sam's lap and kissed her cheek, breaking Sam free from the trance of her dark memories.

"Will you read to me tonight?" Daisy asked.

"Sure, sunshine. You can even read to me, too. We will practice all of the words you know. You're the smartest three year old in the whole world," Samantha gushed as she hugged her girl.

"Hey! I'm almost four, ya know," Daisy said in return as she, too, cuddled into the love-filled embrace.

Sam would do anything to keep that innocent smile on her sweet girl's face. Daisy would know just how cruel the world is soon enough. But for now, Sam would protect that sweet little heart as best as she could.

CHAPTER 6

Carly Chandler sat at her vanity as she undid the pins from her bun and watched the golden locks spill beautifully over her shoulders. She was deep in thought as she applied lotion to her face and combed out the long day out from her hair. She needed to break through Samantha Beckett's walls, but didn't quite know how. Her heart ached with grief as she thought of what poor Samantha's life must be like.

The faded yellow patches of flesh, which covered Sam's arms and face following the phone conference Carly had initiated with Ms. Beckett did not go unnoticed. Carly also knew, all too well, how cruel kids can be and just how alone junior high will make a misunderstood girl feel.

"You okay, babe?" asked Carly's best friend, Todd, as he knocked on the door and leaned against the doorframe of her bedroom.

She turned and smiled at him, the man that rescued her when her own world felt as alone as Samantha's.

"Yes, hon. I'm fine. Just thinking about Samantha."

"You will get through to her, just keep trying," he said as he walked to her, kissed her temple, and squeezed her hand. "There was a time you didn't trust anybody, either. She'll come around. Now get some sleep. Tomorrow morning will be here before you know it, and you need your beauty rest before saving the world," he said, with an understanding smile.

Todd was absolutely perfect in every way. Carly simply did not know what she would do without him in her life, and she told him so often. The two had been inseparable since that cold, rainy night, long, long ago, when the nightmare she had lived for so long finally came to an end. Carly thought she was in love with him in her teenage years, but her gratitude for him and the life he opened up for her had turned that puppy love into a love not yet defined, a love that will thrive until the day that she dies.

Todd loved Carly with equal intensity, however, he worried that their relationship held her back. He wanted nothing but the very best life for his Carly, but her best life was something he was unable to give her. He was happy living the life of a bachelor, in fact, he could never see himself getting married and having a family. But he knew Carly, on the other hand, craved the romantic devotion of a man, of a husband, even though she would never openly admit so. The afternoon that he broke off their teenage romance, in the traditional sense anyway, was the hardest day of his life..

Todd had come out to Carly years before he could say the words to anybody else in an era when being gay was intolerable to both parents, and mainstream society alike. The loyalty, love, and support she offered him in return sealed his love for her eternally, and he would never be fully complete himself until his love, his Carly, lived every day in the happiness that she deserved.

Once Todd left her room, Carly crawled into her plush warm bed and drifted off to sleep with thoughts of gratitude in the comforting softness of her warm sheets. She would show Samantha a new world, a world full of love and endless possibilities...if she could just break through.

CHAPTER 7

The shrill ring of the end-of-period bell startled Samantha into a stiff upright position at her desk, and jolted her from her worry-filled trance. Sam had been consumed with Daisy all day, had been daydreaming about what Daisy was getting into while she was held captive at school. Her episode yesterday, of rummaging through their mother's room to find their storybook, shook Sam to her core. If Daisy gets into trouble while I am at school nobody will be there to save her, she repeated in her head in a constant fear-stricken loop. She knew Daisy's little body could not possibly endure their mothers ever growing and uncontrollable temper.

Sam quickly gathered her books, papers, and large folder, but did not have time to pack them into her backpack. She scooped them off her desk and clumsily carried them in her arms by gripping the cumbersome stack close to her chest, her empty backpack slung over her right shoulder. The class is close to my locker, I can make it, she thought.

Just before she made it to her locker, a group of boys went running past her as they laughed. One of them knocked her in the shoulder and made her books and over-stuffed folder spill out across the hallway floor. She crouched down and frantically tried to pick up all of her papers while heat burned bright pink embarrassment into her cheeks. Please, God, if there is a God, don't let anybody kick my stuff down the hall, she chanted in her head. Just then she saw a fist, full of her papers, reach over her shoulder to help put her things back into their place.

She turned her head, eyes wide with surprise, and was met with Josh Thompson's friendly grin. He helped gather her things and put them back into place, and then left her crouched in the hallway just as quickly as he had appeared, without ever saying a word. Sam stood up in utter shock.

"I see him stare at you."

Sam turned to see Eileen talking to her. She stood speechless. Again.

"You're really pretty, you know. You should try putting on some make-up one day; I can show you how if you want. Have you ever thought about wearing contacts?"

Sam just blinked, put her head down, and walked away. She was not interested in being made fun of right to her face. Whatever tricks they were up to, Sam wanted no part of it. During her walk home Sam remembered the last time she was enticed with false friendship.

"Come over and sit with us, Sam," Amy called out, as she waved her over to the lunch table full of the pretty people.

Sam could hardly believe her ears. She instantly filled with a vibrant cheer that made its way up to her mouth as she beamed a smile at the table of snickering kids. Just as she made her way through the crowded cafeteria to their table, Olivia stuck out her foot and tripped Sam, sending her lunch tray out from her hands as her knees hit the floor. And as she was on all fours, like an unwanted dog, she welled up with tears as she looked at her lunch spilled out in front of her.

As the laughter erupted around her, Sam rose to her feet, ran out of the cafeteria and hid in the stall of the bathroom until the end-of-lunch bell rang. What Sam did not see, however, was how Eileen and Josh looked at each other in disgust with what their friends had just done.

CHAPTER 8

Beth Beckett woke up completely depressed with her miserable life. If only she didn't have children her life would be perfect. That is what she continued to tell herself, anyway. Maybe I can just drive away, make a new life in a new town and leave the brats to fend for them selves. Daisy only loves Samantha, anyway. They wouldn't even know I was gone, she thought.

But no, she couldn't just drive away. Beth was much too selfish for that. Today would begin her devious plan, would begin the process which would rid her life of the burdens she, so undeservingly, had to endure. If she was ever going to live the life she felt entitled to, the life that, because of her children, kept slipping through her grasp, she had to free herself from the heavy chains that bolted her down into her desperate existence. Beth was selfishly evil, a deadly combination with no moral limits, and would do whatever it took to get what she wanted.

She sat on her bed, pulled open her nightstand drawer, and took out a business card folded into a small, discrete square. She opened it and stared at the phone number for a few seconds before dialing them on her phone, then stared blankly into her dresser mirror and grew impatient with each passing ring.

"Hello"

"Hi. This is Beth Beckett."

"It's about time you called," said the man on the other end of the phone. "You've made the right decision."

CHAPTER 9

Thunder boomed through the windows of Sam's last period.

Lovely, she thought. A walk home in the rain. Again.

Springtime storms, which seemed to strike suddenly and then drizzle on endlessly in the Midwest, were unforgiving to a girl that had to walk everywhere, every day. Sam envied her classmates as they ran into the shelter of a waiting car outside of the school, as most parents would never allow their children to trudge home in such stormy conditions.

As she walked home Sam's glasses filled up with water and mist, obscuring her vision almost completely. Don't trip, she thought, as she looked down at the sidewalk drenched in deep puddles, splashing against her bare ankles beneath her staccato steps. The angry wind whipped through her hair and made the thick mass of brown curls stick across her wet face, as if to further her discomfort and disgrace to the highest level of humiliation, as she hurried ahead.

Just get home. Hurry and get home to Daisy. She is waiting for you. She is scared of the thunder, Sam said to herself.

And as she turned the last corner and fought to walk against the wind and rain, as if Mother Nature was shielding Sam from her awaiting nightmare, she squinted to focus on the front room window.

The empty window. Fear gripped Sam's stomach and stopped her breath as she ran up the porch steps and flung open the front door. Her mother was unexpectedly home and sitting in silence on the love seat in the front room. She looked disheveled and undone with mascara tears staining her face, and a cigarette burned to the filter in her hand. Samantha knew in that instant that her world would never be the same.

"Samantha, something's happened. Daisy is gone."

"What do you mean gone!" Shouted Samantha.

"Don't you raise your voice to me, girl," Beth spit out. "Since when do I answer to you? Hmm? I'm waiting...answer me!."

Just then there was a knock on the door. Beth composed herself back into the role of worry-sick mother and opened the heavy front door, stained yellow from years of smoke and nicotine.

"Thank God you're here, Officer," said Beth, as tears filled her eyes once more. "Please come in."

As the man entered the home, Beth shot Sam a look that said a million words in that fleeting second, and Sam understood perfectly. She would keep her mouth shut.

"Ms. Beckett, I'm Detective Brody, and let me assure you I will do whatever it takes to find your daughter. Why don't we start when you realized your daughter...what is her name again?"

"Daisy. My sweet angel, Daisy," Beth sobbed out.

"Daisy. Why don't you tell me when you first noticed Daisy missing from the home."

"I closed my eyes, just for a few minutes, while Daisy was down for her afternoon nap. I woke up surprised that Daisy hadn't come to wake me up with her butterfly kisses like she normally does when I doze off. That's when I got up to check her room and she wasn't there. I searched the house and the backyard but she isn't anywhere!"

"And what time was this, ma'am?" Said Detective Brody.

"Just before I called you, around 2:30. Please, are there other officers out looking for her? She must be cold and scared to death out there!"

"Yes, ma'am. We have units out patrolling the neighborhood. Now tell me. Did you hear or see anything unusual before you fell asleep?"

"No, of course not. I tucked Daisy in for her nap like I always do and then stretched out on the couch to rest my legs for just a few minutes. Do you know how hard I work? Standing on my feet for hours and hours waiting tables just to provide the best life I can for my daughters! I don't think it's too much to ask that I lay down and rest my swollen feet for just a few minutes!"

Brody looked over at Sam, whose head had remained down since he had arrived.

"Of course, Ms. Beckett. Nobody is blaming you. I just need to fit together the pieces of your day leading up to when Daisy went missing, to help bring her home quickly and safely."

Beth quickly gained control of her temper and slipped back into her favorite role of needy woman, the role that always made men do and see what she wanted them to. Only this time it wasn't working which made her rage boil much too close to the surface for her comfort.

"I'm sorry," Beth said to Brody. "I am just sick with worry, forgive my poor manners. But really, I tucked Daisy in, laid down to rest on the couch, and when I woke up she was just gone. I think she has wandered off, as curious children will do, and we are wasting time just sitting here talking.

And with that, just to add more dramatics, she turned her silent tears into sobs as she ran into the bathroom, locked the door, and pretended to get sick.

Brody stood up to see himself out, but just as he opened the front door, he saw Samantha begin to rise from the couch. She looked at the bathroom door to make sure her mother was still locked inside, and then ran straight toward him.

"Daisy is afraid of the thunder," Sam whispered with urgency to the officer.

And then as quickly as she could, Sam ran to her bedroom and sobbed into her pillow with a pain in her heart so sharp, she thought she might die from the intensity of her searing sorrow. She purged her helplessness with each wave of fresh tears, while praying the Detective had understood what she meant. No way would Daisy go outside in this storm, there was just no way, and Sam knew it.

Brody jogged all the way to his car, but still got drenched from the downpour. Once inside he phoned his partner, Detective Jackson, and told him to meet at the station right away. No child would just wander away in this weather Brody thought, as he pulled away from the house. But even he, a seasoned and brilliantly sharp detective, could not yet understand what unspeakable danger Daisy was actually in.

CHAPTER 10

Daisy hugged her legs up close to her chest as she sat on the freezing cold concrete floor, and rested her tiny shoulders against the wall. She was shivering from both fear and the cold, which penetrated through her fragile skin right down to her little bones.

Thunder boomed out again and she sobbed along with the beating rain.

Daisy knew something was strange when her mother had come into her room that afternoon and asked her to come join her for lunch. Beth's voice had a tenderness that Daisy had never heard before, and she was thrilled that her mother finally seemed happy with her. She was getting better at being a good little girl, she thought.

Daisy came bopping out of her room and jumped all the way to the kitchen, hoping her mother would see just how good she was getting at hopping on one foot. She looked up with a smile on her face, but her mother's back was still turned and uninterested in Daisy's accomplishment. Her love-filled heart dimmed a shade as she put her head back down, and walked the rest of the way behind the cold chill her mother left behind.

Daisy reached the kitchen, surprised to see a man and a woman sitting at the table.

"Daisy, don't be so rude," said Beth. "Look up and say hi to your new friends."

"Hello, Daisy. My name is Terry, and this is my wife, Angel. How are you doing today?"

"Good," said Daisy in a small whispered voice.

"Great! How would you like to go on a new adventure today?" Asked Terry.

"Look up when an adult is taking to you, girl," Beth spit out.

Daisy couldn't speak, couldn't move. The man that sat at her kitchen table had eyes darkened with evil and she was completely paralyzed with instinctual fear.

"Well, you're going," said Beth. "Now take this bag and go pack up some of your clothes.

Now!" Shouted her mother at Daisy's inability to move through the fear that cemented her feet to the dirt stained linoleum floor.

Daisy jumped forward at her mother's command, took the large red tote bag into her room, and cried while she picked up her little clothes from the floor and shoved them into the bag.

"Hurry up!" Shouted Beth.

She grabbed her orange doll, hid it in the bottom of the bag, and then walked out slowly in hopes that Samantha would come home to save her before it was too late. Her attempt at stalling did not work.

Daisy was led out to a shiny black car and given a cup of juice once she was buckled in. Maybe this wouldn't be so bad, she thought. As she drank her juice, she began to feel extremely sleepy until she could no longer fight to keep her eyes open and her mind awake. And that was the last thing she remembered. When Daisy woke up, she found herself in this cold cellar, filled with spider webs and dripping cold pipes. There were no windows and a layer of filth covered the entire space.

"Please hurry and find me, Sam. Please. I have to go potty so bad," Daisy cried out, almost silently, as she still felt tired and a little light-headed. She fell asleep once more as tears fell slowly down her chubby little cheeks.

CHAPTER 11

The homeroom bell rang and Ms. Chandler's heart sank as she looked at Samantha's empty desk. Anytime Sam was absent, she worried about what happened in Sam's house to prevent her from coming to school. And as the principal knocked on the classroom door, she was about to find out.

"Ms. Chandler, can you come out to the hallway?" Asked Principle Harris.

"Yes, of course. Class, please work silently until I come back."

"What's going on, Susan?"

"There are two detectives in my office wanting to talk with all of Samantha Beckett's teachers. Her young sister went missing yesterday afternoon."

Carly's hand rose to her mouth. "Oh my God," she said.

"I will watch your class, go down and answer any questions you can for them. And please, keep this quiet for now. I don't want the students disrupted until we know more."

Carly knocked on the cloudy glass window of the Principal's office to alert her arrival, and then opened the door to meet the two men who sat behind Susan's strong oak desk.

This is bad, she thought.

"Please, sit down. Ms. Chandler is it?"

"Yes, sir. Please, call me Carly."

I'm detective Brody, and this is Detective Jackson. As you've heard, Daisy Beckett, Samantha Beckett's little sister, was reported missing yesterday. What can you tell me about the kids and about their mother, Ms. Beckett?"

"Well I've never met Beth in person," said Carly. "But I do know that Samantha takes care of Daisy like she is her own daughter."

"Really?" Said Brody. "That seems like a lot for a young girl to handle. Her mother didn't give me that impression yesterday."

"No, I'm sure she didn't. I have heard she does a good job pretending to be a doting mother when people are around, but most know she's almost never home and that Samantha bears most of the adult responsibilities."

"How do you know that?"

"Well, I came by their house unexpectedly one evening to check on Sam last semester. I could tell something wasn't right at home, and she wouldn't open up to me during school. When I got there Beth wasn't home which, I could tell, was the only reason Sam let me come in. The two girls went about their routine that was so practiced, I knew right away that Samantha was her sister's primary caregiver.

"Did anything strike you as unusual?" Asked Jackson.

"I was surprised to see Samantha as she talked freely and looked happy. She is never like that at school. She was just so tender and loving…

"Why would that be unusual?" Interjected Jackson.

"Because when you're a child who's never received love and kindness, but yet can give the level of love and kindness that I witnessed that day, it's not only unusual, but a miracle if you ask me."

Jackson nodded.

"The house was filthy. I found it almost impossible to breath through the smell of garbage and smoke in every room," Carly continued.

"That house was not suitable living conditions for those kids, and to make matters worse, when I went to the kitchen to wash my hands I found they had no running water."

"Really," said Brody.

"I wanted to scoop those children up and take them home for a hot bath and a decent meal, but I knew I couldn't. So instead, I sat with Sam hoping she would open up to me...she never did, but I had seen enough. I called Child Protective Services the next morning."

Jackson scribbled a note in his flipbook to check the CPS file on the Beckett's home. He flipped the pad closed, tucked his pen back into his pocket, and looked up at Carly.

"Is there anything else you think may help us?"

"Samantha will have the answers for you. Even if she doesn't know she does. But tread lightly with her. After CPS investigated their home and Sam returned to school, I saw her labor in pain with each step she took. She held onto the left side of her ribcage when she thought nobody was looking; I suspect they were beaten and bruised, and God forbid, broken. I tried to ask her about it but she completely shut down, and I knew I would never get through to her in the ways I'd been trying."

"Thank you very much, Ms. Chandler. We will be in touch if we need any more information," said Jackson through the pit in his stomach, a complicated knot from the taut pull of sudden panic.

And with that, Carly walked back to her classroom, and wiped a slow falling tear from her cheek before returning to face her curious class.

CHAPTER 12

Daisy awoke to footsteps above, and wondered who was up there and if they were nice people. She so hoped they were nice and that they would bring her something to eat soon.

Time seemed to be standing still as no light came or went in her dark dungeon, and just as she was about to drift back into sleep, a small bit of light seeped into the small space. Daisy squinted and saw a small door as it opened at the top of an old wooden staircase.

She focused on the tired, sad face and recognized the woman standing there. She was the same lady who had sat at her kitchen table the day before. Daisy smiled up at her, but just as she did, the woman threw her red bag down the steps, followed by two slices of bread, and then quickly turned and slammed the door behind her.

Daisy heard the click of the lock followed by silence once more. She hurried over to her bag with its handles slumped over to the ground, and even in the dark, the bright red fabric contrasted fiercely against the black dirt covering the floor. She dug to the bottom to find her sweet baby doll, and then hugged it close as she promised herself that everything was going to be okay. With her doll gripped in one hand, Daisy picked up the bread with the other and blew off the dirt, looked up to the top of the stairs, and whispered, "thank you".

She ate the bread as fast as she could and wished she had something to drink. Then the pain of her full bladder hit her at once, and made her grip her stomach as she dropped back down to the filthy floor. She started to panic as she stood up once again, looking around to find a safe place to use the bathroom. As she frantically looked from side to side in the dark, she lost control and felt the warmth of her shamefulness run down her legs. A new layer of panic set into her three-year-old mind, as she knew what happened when she had an accident. And the woman upstairs was sure to tell her mother, she just knew it.

Daisy dug through her bag and found new shorts that were faded pink and frayed all along the edges, changed as fast as she could, and then hid her soiled grey leggings in a deep and dark corner behind the steep and scary steps.

CHAPTER 13

S am woke up but could not open her eyes.
They were crusted shut from her evening of
desperate crying. Her tears dried into sticky
glue once she surrendered into the sleep that her
body demanded, as if to keep her mind in the
dark nothingness of her empty desperation.

She was tempted to lie there for the rest of
her life, until God showed her mercy and took her
away from her tortured existence. But she could
not spend another day in bed like she did the day
before. Not until she found Daisy. Not until she
proved her mother was behind her disappearance,
and not until she was able to take Daisy far away
from a future filled with the despair that Sam felt
every single day.

Not knowing what else to do, she crawled out of bed and got ready for school. A sharp pang of emptiness stabbed her heart as she passed by the kitchen and fully realized Daisy was gone, leaving her no reason to set out her sweet baby's breakfast.

I will find you Daisy, just stay strong, Sam thought to herself.

She made her way into homeroom just before the final bell rang. She took her seat and instantly felt she had made a mistake by coming to school. There was no way she was going to be able to sit still while listening to her teachers drag on and on about things that just didn't matter right now. As she was forming an excuse to escape the classroom in her head, there was a knock at the door.

Ms. Chandler looked at Sam with worry and sadness, then walked over and greeted Principal Harris. They spoke briefly, and then Ms. Chandler said, "Samantha, Mrs. Harris would like to speak with you in her office."

"Ooooh!" cried some of the other students in unison. "Somebody is in trouble!"

Not now! Samantha thought, I don't have time for this right now!

As they reached the office, Mrs. Harris turned and said, "Samantha, Detective Brody is in my office and would like to speak to you about Daisy."

They walked in, and there was Brody sitting behind the desk, looking as strong and trustworthy as the dark oak desk supporting his elbows.

"Hello Samantha, thank you for coming down."

"Sure," she said, as she thought, what choice did I have.

"How are things at home, Samantha?" asked Brody.

"Fine."

"Fine?" Said Brody. "You don't look fine."

Samantha kept her head down.

"Sam. I am here to help you, to help bring your sister home safely, so any information you have will help us in our efforts to bring Daisy home to you."

Brody calculated his words carefully, hoping he would come through to Sam by pleading with her need to have Daisy home for her only, and not for their mother. His tactic worked.

"All I know is when I came home my mother was crying, saying something happened, and that Daisy was gone."

Brody quickly jotted a note. "Something happened? What happened?"

"I don't know. When I tried to ask what she was talking about she became furious, and that's when you knocked on the door."

"What do you think she meant?"

"I have no idea."

"What did your mother say after we left?"

"I haven't spoken to her since before you came over. I went straight to my room and she has been gone ever since." Brody jotted down another note. His writing down what she was saying was making her uncomfortable. No, more than uncomfortable. His documenting her words made her tremble with a low burning terror, threatening to strangle the little breath she had left in her throat.

"I shouldn't be here, I should get back to class," said Sam, as her legs began to tremble underneath her clammy hands, hands that were gripping her knees and trying to force her nerves to obey.

"We're almost done, Sam," Brody said, as he looked at her with eyes filled with love, filled with understanding, and filled with sweet patience.

Sam lost herself in his eyes for a moment. They were big and round, which complemented his strong cheekbones and large straight nose. Their green color was deep, mixed with rich shades of brown that popped when the light hit them in just the right way, as they did now with the morning sun rising through the back office window. The brown in his eyes matched his light brown hair perfectly.

"Sam?"

Sam snapped back into the conversation as her cheeks filled with color, embarrassed for daydreaming in the warmth of his eyes.

"I am here to help you, Sam. I will do everything I can to reunite you with your sister, but I need your help. You are the key to unlock what has happened to her."

And in that moment Sam trusted him, wholeheartedly.

"I know my mother did something," she sobbed. "I just don't know what. Please help me," Sam released all at once. And she instantly felt better, felt hopeful, and felt like she may see her sister again after all.

———————◆———————

"Sam! Wait up!"

Sam turned to see Eileen jogging toward her in the crowded hallway.

"Hey, I have been trying to talk to you all day, but you keep walking away. I might just start to get offended," Eileen said with a smile.

"Hey, yeah. Sorry. What do want?"

"Want? I don't want anything, really. My mom told me about Daisy and the Amber Alert last night. All the news channels are talking about her going missing, and I wanted to make sure you're okay."

"Okay. Yeah, I'm okay."

"Come on, Sam. We used to be friends."

"Not since third grade," Sam said flatly.

"But still. I miss all the laughs we used to have. Come over after school, let me help you with Daisy."

"I'm sorry, I can't," said Sam. "I have to go."

And with that Sam left Eileen standing alone in the middle of the hall, as Ms. Chandler watched from her door with a smile on her face.

Progress Carly thought. I see progress.

CHAPTER 14

Sam walked home with a renewed sense of hope. Detective Brody believed her, and Sam knew he would find Daisy and make things right.

She hurried home to do exactly as he had instructed her to do. Now she could only pray that her mother wasn't home when she got there.

Sam quietly walked through the door and was hit by the potent sting of Beth's cheap perfume, its scent filling her nose and mouth which made her breathe in short and shallow breaths. She tiptoed down the hall and saw an empty bathroom, along with her mother's bedroom door that was shut and locked. She was alone and she was grateful, so much so, her eyes filled to the brim with tears. Only now her hot and comforting tears were in response to Sam's overwhelming relief, and not the convenient store perfume hanging thickly throughout the house.

This was exactly what Sam had hoped for. Beth had obviously just left, which gave Sam time to look through her mother's things and lessened the chance of getting caught. She needed to find a clue, anything to lead Detective Brody to Daisy before she was gone forever.

Sam hurried to the kitchen and got a butter knife out of the sink to jimmy open her mother's door. As she tried to pop open the lock, she paused a moment to calm her nerves and slow down. Rushing could cause an indent in the soft wood frame and give away her investigation. Slowly, she placed the knife in between the doorframe and the latch once more, and applied deliberate pressure until the latch depressed into the cylinder of the handle and popped the door wide open.

Sam's heart raced with a mix of fear and exhilaration. I actually did it, she thought.

Slowly she entered the room and laid the knife on her mother's bed. She looked around, frozen in the dark energy of the room, and calculated where to start when she didn't even know what she was looking for. Detective Brody said she would just know what it was when she found it—anything that seemed out of place. She laughed to herself, the only thing out of place in her mother's life is Daisy and me, Sam thought.

She carefully opened her mother's dresser drawers and gingerly looked through her clothes. The top drawer was filled with the most beautiful lace and silk she had ever seen, and she envied all of her mother's fancy underwear. Samantha had outgrown all of her underwear years ago, and Daisy had never even owned any of her own.

Sam lay on the floor to look under her mother's bed. There was nothing there except a baseball bat her mother kept for protection, in case one of her boyfriends tried to hurt her. Sam rolled her eyes and wondered why her mother kept trying to date when all of the men she brought home ultimately left her, in which she always blamed Sam or Daisy for not being good enough kids.

"You drove him away!" She would always say.

The ones that left Beth were the good ones, though. The bad ones were violent, and even though Sam wished she could enjoy seeing Beth on the other end of a ruthless beating, she was too frightened that the men would tire of their mother and move on to her and Daisy. It had happened before.

Sam pushed the thought from her head and moved on to the nightstand. There was a creased up business card lying on top of all the junk inside of the drawer. On the back was written "Daisy" with a phone number underneath her name. The front of the card said, "Loving Home Adoption Agency" and underneath that it said, in italics, "All children deserve a place to call home."

Sam's heart began to race and she felt sick.

"Adoption? No! Daisy has a place to call home, here with me!" Sam screamed into the deafening silence of her empty house.

She composed herself and looked carefully through the rest of the drawer, but did not find anything else suspicious. Knowing that she couldn't take the card without her mother noticing, she ran to her room, flipped up her mattress and dug into the hole she cut underneath to hide her homemade journal and pen. She quickly returned to her mother's room and wrote down all of the information on the card. There wasn't much, just the name of the agency along with their website, and what her mother had hand written on the back.

She was getting more and more furious with each passing second. Once her journal was tucked safely back into her hiding space, she stomped back to her mother's closet and flung open the french doors. The abundance of clothes, neatly hung, made Sam's temper rage, as she thought of how little her poor Daisy had. She dug through the shoes, making sure to place each one back where she had picked it up, but found nothing except several bottles of expensive shampoo and conditioner that Beth kept hidden from her children.

What a bitch, Samantha thought.

Just as she was about to close the closet doors she looked up and saw a box with a green clover stamped on the outside, which matched the ominous boxes she had found in the attic. She knew right away those attic boxes held secrets that, at the time, she wanted no part of. But now her mother's actions left her no choice but to discover the truth.

CHAPTER 15

Carly Chandler came home and paced around her living room. She had to do something. She wanted desperately to go to the Beckett home and hug Sam until she felt the power that a loving touch can bring; and she wanted to help in the search for Daisy, but did not know how or where to start.

She picked up her purse and keys several times to drive over to Samantha, but memories of her own childhood, and the memories of an angry abusive mother kept stopping her. She did not want to be the cause of Beth's temper again, knowing Sam would receive that fury all over her body until her mother's rage was completely emptied.

The thought of that had trapped Carly in her own dark, childhood existence.

"Carly! Who the hell are you talking to! Hang up that phone right now, girl!"

Carly hung up the phone, as her heart raced in her throat. She didn't hear her mother come in, and was not expecting her home for hours or else she never would have answered the phone when it rang.

As she lowered the phone back to the receiver, she heard Todd say, "Wait!"

"Answer me."

Her mother's voice was low and calm, which was a really bad sign.

"I was talking to a friend from school, mom" Carly replied.

"A friend? You don't have any friends. Nobody from school would call an ugly, stupid girl like you. Now you have one last chance to answer my question. Who in hell were you talking to?"

Carly's mind raced to find an answer that would satisfy her mother and prevent what she already knew was inevitable.

She waited too long.

"Are you trying to call the police, again? You are dumber than I thought. Don't learn very well, do you."

With each word, her mother walked closer and closer as her temper bubbled to the surface, ready to explode with furious punches into Carly's stomach.

Carly was fighting to keep quiet as her mother's blows hit her, one after the other. But when her mother yanked her off the bed by her hair and kicked in her ribs, she cried out in pain as she heard the crack of her bones and felt fire fill her lungs. I am going to die, she thought. And I never even got to kiss Todd.

What Carly, nor her mother, knew was that the phone did not click into the receiver. Her new friend, her savior, had heard everything. She had just begun to trust him and shared with him, just a little, about her mother's insanity, and now Todd fully understood Carly's torture.

That very night, Todd and his parents showed up at their front door with the police. Her mother could not talk her way out of her abuse this time, and Carly was taken into protective custody, and then later went to live with Todd and his family. His parents showed her, for the first time, what it was like to live with love and with the complete absence of fear. Carly's only wish was that somebody had stepped up before she was sixteen years old and saved her sweet childhood sooner.

She broke free from her memory and drove straight to the police station to talk to Detective Brody, and urge him to remove Samantha from her mother's entrapment before another child was lost right before her eyes.

CHAPTER 16

Brody was on the phone at his desk which was topped with a mound of files and paperwork. He stood up with a direct urgency as he hung up the phone, and grabbed his suit coat from the back of his chair.

The Department of Human Services had shed crucial light on the history of Beth Beckett, and the case of Daisy's disappearance took an ominous turn. An emergency arrest warrant was granted, along with the order to remove Samantha Beckett from her mother's care immediately.

As Brody gathered the required paperwork off the fax machine, he saw Carly Chandler walk through the door.

"Detective Brody" said Carly. "Can I talk to you please?"

"I don't have time, Ms. Chandler. I am heading out right now."

Carly could see the worry on his face.

"Is this about Daisy? That is what I need to talk to you about. I'm afraid Samantha is in serious danger."

"I am headed over to the Beckett home now, but I can't tell you anything more," replied Brody.

"Has something happened? Please Detective. I need your help getting Samantha out of that house before something happens to her. I know women like Beth, my mother WAS a woman like Beth."

Carly's voice began to tremble and rise to a feverish and pleading pitch.

"I know first hand the danger Sam is in, and what her mother will surely do to her once she finds out she spoke with you today!"

Brody saw the helpless terror on Carly's face and he softened.

"I am meeting Child Protective Services at the Beckett home right now. She is being removed from Ms. Beckett's care to be placed into protective custody of the state."

"Let me take her!" Shouted Carly. My house is a licensed foster home. Please, after all she has been through, I think it's crucial she at least be placed with somebody she knows. Somebody that knows her history and can help her once the details of Daisy's disappearance come to light."

"Your house is already licensed?" asked Brody, as Carly followed behind him through the front door of the station, and down the front steps.

"Yes, before I began teaching full-time I was a foster parent. I've always been called to help children in need, to be a soft place to land once the only world they know has been turned upside-down. Please, place Samantha in my care, nobody could possibly care more."

"Okay Ms. Chandler. Follow me to the Beckett home. I'll let CPS know you're coming, and that my recommendation is for Samantha to be released into your care."

"Thank you so much."

And slowly, Carly felt the vice which gripped her heart start to release, just a little.

CHAPTER 17

Sam stood in the closet and stared up at the box while the box seemed to stare back at her, begging her to open up its secrets. Secrets hidden for far too long.

She went to the kitchen to get a chair and then placed it in the closet after moving aside the full rack of clothes. She climbed up, stretched up on her tiptoes, and reached until she had the box in her hands. She slowly opened the side flaps and looked inside with one hand, as the other balanced the weight. On top was a photo album. She began flipping through the pictures and recognized her mother in all of them. She was smiling and laughing, and seemed lit up with her life. She had never seen her mother look so carefree. A man was also in most of the photos with her, and he had the same radiating blue eyes that stared back at Sam in the mirror every day. She found herself feeling a pang of sadness that she did not understand, and then realized she was likely looking at her own father.

But it couldn't be. He looked so happy, his image felt so warm. Her mother had told her, since she could remember, that her father was a worthless, evil man that had left her while pregnant with their child. She said he was stupid and weak, but this man looked nothing like that.

The very last picture in the album was this blue eyed man and her mother, and on the man's lap was a young child whom looked about three years old. The life she saw in her mother's eyes from the previous pictures was gone, and replaced with a face which looked both depressed and slightly vicious. The man, on the other hand, was glowing with a radiant smile as he looked down upon the child, as the girl looked back up at him in complete adoration.

Samantha stared at the photograph. The little girl in the picture was neither her, nor Daisy. As she looked closer she saw so much of Daisy in this child, the same nose, the same dimple in her smile, and the same big round eyes. The only difference was this little girl had curly brown hair, much like Samantha's.

Samantha shut the album as chills covered her entire body, and the hair stood up on her arms and neck.

Underneath the photo album Samantha found miscellaneous letters and cards, and a marriage certificate with the names Arlene Arnold and Chad Beckensworth typed in. But she was drawn to Arlene's signature. That signature was penned with handwriting she knew all too well. Her mother had signed the marriage certificate, but who was Arlene Arnold, thought Sam, as the confusion in her head was making her dizzy. So much so, she momentarily lost her footing on the chair and nearly dropped the box to the ground.

After she braced herself and took a few deep breaths, she looked further. She found an old birth certificate with the same name, Arlene Arnold. Signed the same year her mother was born, from the same city in Kentucky where her mother had once told her she grew up. The disclosure stood out to Sam because her mother never discussed her life before she had children, as if Beth's very existence began only once Sam was born.

She placed everything back into the box as she had found them, folded the flaps of the top back together, and reached up to place the box back on the top shelf. As she closed the closet doors, closed and locked her mother's door, and returned the chair back to the kitchen, she decided she absolutely had to uncover what was in those attic boxes, had to uncover who her mother was and had to find out who the child in the haunting photograph was. More than those things though, she needed to find out who she was.

CHAPTER 18

As evening drew near, Daisy's silent tears turned to soft whimpers. She felt the pang of her hunger burn through her stomach, as the desperation for water made her nauseous. She was becoming so dehydrated that even her tears had dried up, making her eyes scratch with pain every time she blinked.

"Sam." Daisy whimpered over and over.

"I'm sorry I wasn't a good girl while you were away at school. I'm sorry I took your book from mommy's room. I didn't mean to be bad. I tried really, really hard to be good."

Daisy was talking to herself, hoping that wherever Sam was, she could hear her pleas for forgiveness and come to keep her safe and warm.

"Please don't cry, dolly," Daisy said to her doll as she clutched it close to her chest.

"We will be okay. Sam will find us, she promised she would keep us safe. She never lies, not like Mommy. Sam will come get us. I never lie, either, dolly. She will come get us and bring us dinner, and then maybe she can live down here with us, too."

Daisy rocked back and forth, as it the eased the pain in her stomach and spine, which ached from the constant shivers that shook through her body.

Suddenly the door at the top of the stairs flung open from a forceful kick and Daisy felt instant terror. The man at the top of the steps pulled a long string and flooded the basement with light, which burned Daisy's eyes, and made her bury her face into her baby doll.

"Hi, there Daisy" said Terry in a voice full of fake softness.

"Are you hungry? I brought you something to eat."

Daisy kept her face buried in the comfort of her doll.

"Your mom was right, you really don't mind your manners at all."

Daisy slowly looked up and squinted until her eyes adjusted to assault of light, which shone upon her dark confinement. She saw past the scary man and zoned in on the plate of food; a sandwich made of bread and cheese, and a glass of water.

She nearly lunged at the plate, but fear kept her body still.

"Would you like this dinner, Daisy?"

Daisy shook her head yes, still unable to use her voice.

"Well you have to do a few things for me first. That's only fair, don't you think?"

Daisy shook her head in agreement once more.

"Get up and give Uncle Terry a hug. Don't just sit there, I won't hurt you. I just want a hug from a sweet little girl."

Reluctantly, Daisy rose and walked into the man's outstretched arms. He embraced her and held her tight, while his thumb traced down her back.

"See, that wasn't so bad, was it?"

Daisy shook her head no, while looking down at the floor as she fought back the urge to run and cry.

"Now, see that broom over there in the corner? I need you to get that broom, and sweep up all the dirt into one big pile. This is where you will be staying for a little while, until Uncle Terry finds you a new place to live since your mommy couldn't handle you anymore."

Those words stung and Daisy began to weep from the terror that filled her chest, strangling her neck without mercy.

"No crying now, Daisy. You may not have been a good little girl for your mother, but you will be a good little girl for me. Now go get that broom and start sweeping. Unless, that is, you like sleeping in the dirt like a filthy little pig?"

"No, sir," Daisy finally got out.

She went to the broom and picked it up, struggling with the weight, as the broomstick was much taller than her. As she looked around the cellar for the first time in the light, she realized her prison was much scarier than she had imagined.

There were heavy chains with handcuffs attached to the ends bolted to the floor in the dusty corner to the right of the steps, and now she could see that fat spiders occupied the webs she saw on her first night there

"You don't want me to put those chains on you, do you?"

"No, sir."

"Good, I didn't think so. I just know you are going to listen to everything Uncle Terry tells you to do. And don't you worry about those spiders, they will help keep you warm at night," he laughed, as Daisy's face curled up with a fresh wave of horror.

Daisy struggled to sweep as best she could. She had never swept a floor before, but she had seen Sam do it many times. It was a lot harder than it looked, though. She kept stopping from the pain of her hunger, but every time she did so, Uncle Terry laughed at her. So she tried her best to stay upright through the sharp stabs in her stomach, and finish her chore. She had a feeling a mad Uncle Terry was a lot worse than a mad Mom.

"Good girl. Now come sit on my lap and eat your dinner."

Daisy ran to the plate and sat in his lap. She reacted so fast to his command, and to her demanding stomach, that once she finished the sandwich she couldn't remember why or how she was on his lap. But she wanted off immediately.

"Wow, maybe you really are a little pig" chuckled Terry. Now drink your water he said, with an evil grin on his face."

The water tasted funny, like her juice when she was in his fancy car. But she was so thirsty she could not stop gulping it down. Then, before she knew it, she was falling asleep as Terry placed her on the ground in front of the steep steps.

"Keep being a good girl, Daisy, and tomorrow I will bring you a pillow and blanket to sleep with. Tomorrow, pretty girl, is when your fun will really begin." Terry said, as he walked up the stairs and through the little door.

CHAPTER 19

Sam slowly crawled up the shelves in her closet and pushed open the door that sealed off the mysteries trapped above. She pushed the cobwebs out of her way and hoisted herself up, while her heart raced with fear filled anticipation. She pulled the metal string, only to hear the pop of the light bulb as it went out, keeping dark shadows upon the space.

"Damn-it" she said.

Just as fear began to push Sam out of her confinement, she saw a flashlight.

She bargained with herself. If the flashlight works, I will continue, she thought. She clicked the button. Light. "Okay, be brave. Be brave for Daisy," Sam whispered.

She crawled over to the boxes and took down the first of three that were stacked on top of each other. It was lighter than she was expecting and her anxiety calmed a little. *What was I expecting, to find the little girl up here?* She thought as she shook her head.

She opened up the box and shined the light inside.

She saw more letters and cards, doodled with hearts and promises of forever love. She picked up the letter on top and held it with both hands, as she balanced the flashlight between her chin and chest.

"Dear Chad,

I have prayed for your safe return from Iraq everyday, and I ache for your touch and embrace every night. I pray that God makes you understand we need each other, that you realize I am the only woman for you, and that even the distance of the ocean will not keep you from me. So imagine my surprise to learn you have already returned to Kentucky. That you have been home for months. How do you think that makes me feel? Me, who has stayed devoted to you in every way? How do you think it makes me feel when you will not return my phone calls?

I will be here waiting for you, Chad. I hope to see you soon.

Yours forever,
Arlene."

Sam stared at the paper. This was her mother's handwriting alright, but why was she calling herself Arlene, she thought, as she pulled out the next letter. This one from Chad.

"Arlene,

I received your letter. I told you before my deployment that it was over between us. I am sorry I do not feel the same for you, as you do for me. Please move on, because I have.
Best Regards,
Chad."

Sam was mesmerized by the story of these two people, strangers that felt so familiar to her. She kept reading, one letter after the other, still wondering where the little girl from the picture came from.

"My Dearest Chad,

I told you we were only meant for one another. I saw it in your eyes when I came calling to your mother's house. You couldn't turn me away, could you? When you saw my tears while telling me to move on, you understood. Why else would you wipe those tears from my cheeks with the softness of your thumb? You will thank me for keeping us together. You will see.

Yours Always,
Arlene."

"Arlene,
Please, you must leave me alone. I am sorry I
confused you when you came to my home. I had a
moment of weakness, which was not fair to you. I
do not love you. Please, move on. You will make
some man, somewhere, very happy one day. It just
won't be me.
—Chad."

"My Sweet Chad,
I am sorry I have to tell you this through a
letter, but you will not see me, nor take my calls. I
am pregnant. See? It was not a moment of
weakness, but a moment orchestrated by God.
Come home to me. We are going to be a family.
Love Always,
Arlene."

"I have a sister," said Sam. "An older
sister." She had to stop reading and catch her
breath.

At the bottom of the box were more
pictures of these two people. At first her mother
looked happy, but as she continued through the
images she saw that happiness fade and the

twisted scowl that she knows so well, began to emerge.

She stopped at a photo of Chad kissing her mother's swollen belly. Such a happy moment filled with the anticipation of a new life almost ready to join the world. But Sam was stuck on her mother's face. A face filled with jealousy and disgust. She picked up the stack of letters once more and began to read.

"Chad,

I can see you love Jennifer more than you love me. How can this be? I gave you that gift of a daughter, and I can take it away just as easily. Come home to me.

—Arlene."

"Arlene,

What do you mean take her away from me? She is safe here with me, and the court agreed. Stop your threats.

"Chad.*"

"My Love,

I am pregnant again. You have two choices: Come home and make us a family as we ought to be, or don't. But if you don't, I will move out of state and you will never see me again. You will never find this new baby of ours, and I will tell her, everyday

of her life, that it is your selfish fault that she doesn't have a daddy.
—Arlene."

"You win.
—Chad."

And that was the last of the letters. Sam began to black out as her anxiety grabbed ahold of her body, and made her teeter on the edge of passing out. She closed her eyes for a moment and then took deep, deliberate breaths until her vision came into focus once more.

She moved onto the second box, picking it up from the place it had occupied for more than 10 years. As she began opening the flaps, the flashlight fell to the floor and revealed a rat, just as it was scampering away to find a new hiding place.

Tears filled Sam's eyes, while her nausea pressed her forward with a new sense of urgency.

This box was filled with old newspaper clippings from her mother's hometown. She picked up the first one she saw, and read the headline.

<u>Little girl still missing, mother a person of interest</u>

The next read:

Father urges community to continue its search

And the last one she read out loud, as she tried to steady her shaking hands:

Remains of child confirmed as Jennifer Beckensworth

Sam threw the yellowed clippings back into the box, and hurled it across the attic. She tore open the third box and found an old teddy bear, a child's red polka dot dress, and a wedding ring that looked to have been smashed by a hammer. She pulled out the dress and shined the flashlight directly on it. The material was stiff and crusty, and as she shined the light on the lace trimmed collar, she saw it was covered in old, rust colored blood.

"No!" She screamed, right before she succumbed to her swirling head and passed out.

CHAPTER 20

Beth pulled into her driveway in her brand new, cherry red, mustang convertible. She looked at the front door and rolled her eyes with pure resentment at having to come home. She knew if she stayed away from her house, and Samantha, she would come under suspicion. She knew she had to play this game for a little while, and knew how to play the game all too well.

She was already preparing for her supreme performance, explaining how and why she purchased a new car in the midst of Daisy's search and rescue operation to the police. But she just couldn't wait! Her new found riches were begging to be spent, and she deserved the splurge, did she not? She walked around to the back seat and gathered up all of her shopping bags. Her purse strap fell off her shoulder and onto her arm, its weight making her lose footing and drop the bags that were clutched in her hand.

Beth kept her temper in check, as the neighbors were out and looking at her with suspicion. Even though she wanted to scream, 'mind your own *fucking* business' she smiled sweetly at them instead. "Retail therapy," she laughed with a small shrug of her shoulders as she walked into the house.

"Sam, get out here and help me."

She received only silence in return.

Where is that girl? Beth thought, as her temper began to fill up her throat. She put her bags in front of her locked bedroom door before going to search through the house. If that lazy ass is sleeping in the middle of evening, she is going to get it, thought Beth, as she flung open Sam's door. But her bed was empty. She checked Daisy's room, and then the bathroom.

"Oh, Sam. Stupid, stupid Sam. Just wait until you get home," Beth said, as she dug in the bottom of her purse for the key to her bedroom.

She pushed open her door with her shoulder as she gathered up her new treasures. Her anger subsided as she began daydreaming about her new man, and how impressed he would surely be with her new clothes, and hot new car.

She cracked a wicked smile as she felt the blood begin to pulse between her legs, just before she stopped dead in her tracks.

She dropped the bags to the floor as she zoned in on the butter knife sitting on the edge of her bed.

She hurried over to the nightstand and ripped open the drawer. There was the card, still sitting where she had left it. Nothing else appeared out of place but Beth's fury raged anyway.

She screamed a loud primal scream, like an enemy soldier running into battle to decimate their opposition.

———————◆———————

Foggy headed, Sam opened her eyes as her mother's scream rang louder and louder in her ears. She blinked as she sat up and instantly remembered where she was, snooping in the attic, which was forbidden. She pulled her knees into her chest and began to sob as she clutched the blood-soiled dress. Her mother would find her here. Daisy had surely met the same fate as little Jennifer, and today would be her last day on earth as well, she thought, as her sobs echoed out louder and louder. She did not care if her mother heard though; it was the only way to be with Daisy forever.

Sam could not bear one more single second of her misery and begged God to take her away before her mother found her. Either way she would soon be in Heaven, so she sat and waited, and cried out her desperation. In fact, she released her sobs with such intensity that she did not hear her mother's footsteps barreling down the hall and into her room. Nor did she hear her mother climb up her closet shelving and reach up into her cocoon.

"You stupid, ungrateful bitch!"

Sam did not look up but felt her mother's hand twist into her hair, and with one swift yank, she tumbled down onto her closet floor. Her arm hit the ground first, and as if in slow motion, the rest of her body followed, filling Samantha's ears with the crack of her arm splitting in two beneath her own weight.

She held her head back and howled to the ceiling, with tears and sweat streaming down her face.

"Please God! Take me! Please!" Sam screamed through her unbearable pain.

"God doesn't love worthlessness, and that's what you are!" Beth bellowed, as she dragged Sam out of the closet by her broken arm, until her shoulder popped out of its socket, searing a new level of pain throughout Sam's entire body.

"Sit up" said Beth.

Sam lay still on her bedroom floor, looking past her mother and wishing for death to release her from her pain.

"I said sit the fuck up" spat Beth, just before she kicked in Sam's ribs, filling the hate-filled space with the sound of cracking bones and Sam's animalistic wail.

CHAPTER 21

Carly pulled up to the Beckett home shortly behind Detective Brody and parked her car in front of the house. She grabbed her purse from the passenger seat and headed toward Brody's car. She slowed down and then came to a complete stop as she saw the brand new car in the driveway.

"No. Way."

Brody reached over the center console to open the passenger side door.

"Come on in, Ms. Chandler. The caseworker from the CPS office should be here any minute."

"Whose car is that? Shouldn't we go in right away? What if Sam is in danger!"

"That" said Brody, "is Ms. Beckett's new car. I ran the plates as soon as I got here."

"What?" Exclaimed Carly. "I don't understand. A new car? Now? That doesn't make any sense!"

As Carly eased into the deep bucket seat of Brody's car, his hand lightly brushed over the top of hers as he slid back over to the driver's side. Her heart slammed into her chest as electricity shot through her hand and straight down the rest of her body. Before Carly had time to process what had just jolted through her core, they heard a wild scream; the kind of scream fueled by imminent danger and immense pain. They both flew out of the car and ran up the driveway. Brody told Carly to stand back as he raised his leg and kicked in the door with one solid thrust of his weight.

"Stay Back!" Brody screamed at Carly.

"Police!"

Brody had his weapon raised as he rushed to the sound of Sam's wails.

"Beth, get away from that girl and get your hands up," screamed Brody as he pointed his gun toward her.

Beth didn't say a word. She glared at Sam crumpled on the ground with disgust, and then began cackling uncontrollably. Oh this isn't over, girl, oh no it is not, she thought as she slowly turned to face Brody with her hands above her head.

Brody quickly approached her, grabbed her arms, and cuffed her hands tightly behind her back. He threw her onto Sam's bed as he radioed into the station for an ambulance.

"Sam, honey. You are going to be okay. Don't close your eyes, stay with me. The ambulance is on its way."

Sam saw Ms. Chandler racing into the room. Once Carly was by Sam's side, Brody picked Beth up off the bed, read her rights, and ushered her out the door with one hand gripped tightly around her upper arm and the other held firmly at her back.

"The attic..." Sam whispered out toward Brody, just before unconsciousness took her once more.

CHAPTER 22

Just as the ambulance drove away with Samantha safely inside, Carly by her side, two units of police officers arrived, followed by two federal agents with the FBI.

Two of the uniformed policemen took Beth into custody while the remaining two began searching the Beckett home. The FBI agents approached Brody with their handshakes ready, and introduced themselves.

"Detective, this is Agent Cooper, and I'm Special Agent Townsend," said the older of the two men, as he shook Brody's hand and showed his FBI badge. The two men were opposites in every way. Townsend stood an intimidating 6 foot, 5 inches tall, with broad shoulders that looked as if they could once carry the weight of the world. His salt and peppered hair, along with his belly, which protruded above his belt from years of his wife's home cooking, gave away his retirement age. Cooper, however, was young and fresh, squeaky clean some might say. He was short and thin with crisp blond hair buzzed closely around his ears, which accentuated their unusually large size in comparison to his small head, and tiny, but sincere, blue eyes.

Townsend wasted no time explaining the reason for their sudden arrival.

"Our department has been searching for Mrs. Arlene Beckensworth since she fled Kentucky almost twelve years ago with her infant daughter, Samantha, at which time she was under investigation for the murder of her eldest child, Jennifer, as well as for the disappearance of her husband, Chad Beckensworth."

"We received a tip," said Agent Cooper, "that she was living here in Michigan under the alias Beth Beckett from the local Child Protection Services office."

"We arrived in town this evening, and your superior briefed us on the current situation," said Townsend.

As the three men talked in front of the steps to the Beckett home, Brody's partner Jackson finally arrived.

"What took you so long?" said Brody. "Never mind," he said impatiently. "This is agent Cooper and Townsend with the FBI, and they've been tracking Mrs. Arlene Beckensworth's whereabouts for some time now."

"I discovered Beth Beckett was actually Arlene this afternoon from the Department of Human Services," said Jackson. "They pieced it together after CPS was called late last year to investigate the Beckett home. Unfortunately, there was a miscommunication between the two channels, and that information sat undiscovered until I contacted CPS for information to aid in our current missing child investigation."

"Looks like we arrived here just in time," said Brody. "Follow us, we'll help each other fill in the blanks, as I'm afraid we have little time," and even less hope, he thought, "to find Daisy alive."

The four men entered the Beckett home, one after the other, in a suit-coated uniformed line, before dispersing throughout the house to look for clues.

"Detective Brody, we found this in Ms. Beckett's room," said one of the uniformed officers, as he handed him the adoption agency's card.

Brody looked at the back and immediately called the phone number written under Daisy's name.

The number you are trying to reach is temporarily disconnected, said the recording through the earpiece. Brody shook his head no to the officer. "Not in service. Run the number and see what you can find." The officer penned the number in his notepad before returning to the bedroom.

"Jackson!" yelled Brody.

Jackson rushed into the living room, followed by the federal agents.

"Take a look at this."

Jackson took the card and read it out-loud. "Loving Home Adoption Agency. All Children Deserve a Place to Call Home."

"Let me see that," said Townsend. "Not very much information on here, but things just got interesting."

"Look at the back," said Brody flatly.

As Townsend read Daisy's name out loud, the newly formed team of men felt a sense of hope that they may find Daisy alive after all, though you could not tell so by their expressionless faces.

"Well that explains the new car in the driveway," said Agent Cooper.

Townsend explained, "Child Trafficking Rings often operate under the guise of a legal adoption agency. They target and solicit women like Arlene, or Beth if you will, and offer top dollar to "place" their children within their agency. Some mothers are duped by their desperate circumstances, while others find it a convenient answer to their problems."

"Based on Beth's past, my guess for her is the latter," said Brody. No dirty work, no body, and no murder investigation trailing her again."

"I'm afraid Daisy's fate is worse off with these people," said Townsend as he held up the card, "then it was under her mother's care, even as bad as it was. These rings operate nationwide, and there is a good chance if Daisy is with them, she will be taken out of state soon, if she hasn't been already. We need to act now."

The two FBI agents followed Brody back to the station, while Jackson stayed behind to oversee the rest of the search. His face was twisted with fury from the stupidity of Beth Beckett. Luckily for him the rest of the team missed his rising temper in their rush to return to the station. Jackson took great pride in his professionalism. He pulled himself together to finish what he had come to the house to do.

CHAPTER 23

Sam slowly blinked her eyes as she came back into consciousness, confused with the constant beep she heard in steady repetition coming from behind her. She winced in pain as she looked at her cast-covered arm, and then to the IV placed into the top of her hand on the other arm. Slowly her memory returned as she realized where she was. And that she was still alive.

"No," she whispered out as she began to cry. "Daisy."

Carly, who had fallen asleep in the old vinyl visitor's chair next to Sam's bed, woke up with a jolt and quickly grabbed Samantha's hand.

"Ms. Chandler?" asked Sam. "What are you doing here?"

"Hi Sam," Carly replied with genuine care and enthusiasm. "How are you feeling?"

Sam just lay back down and turned her head away.

"Sam," said Carly as she lightly squeezed her hand, "I am here for you. For whatever you need." She received only silence in return.

"You don't have to talk now, but I will be here when you're ready."

"I am never going to be ready," said Sam. "And don't say you're here for me, because nobody is. Not even God. I begged Him to take me away from my pain, to take me home to my Daisy. But here I am. Still here. Still in pain. Still without the only good thing I ever had in my life."

"Why do you think Daisy is dead?" asked Carly. "The police are looking for her, sweetheart. We don't know where she is yet, but we can't lose hope."

"Never mind. I don't want to talk about it. I just want to go home. When can I go home?"

"The doctor said you will be discharged in the morning, and then you get to come home with me."

"Why!" yelled Sam. I don't want to go home with you, I just want to go home."

"Your mother has been arrested, Sam, and you have been removed from her custody. You can't live at home by yourself—"

"Oh yes I can!" shouted Sam. "I've lived by myself my whole life!"

"I know you have, Sam. I really do know. I know better than you think."

Just then the nurse came into the room to administer another dose of morphine to help Sam with her pain, and to help her sleep through the night.

"Can I get you anything, Ms. Chandler? Another pillow, or some water?" said the nurse.

"No, I am just fine, thank you."

And with that Carly curled into her chair, pulled the blanket up to her chin, and prayed that Sam would accept her home and her love as she tried to fall asleep.

———— ◆ ————

Sam woke before sunrise and sat in the stillness, with only the sound of her beeping monitors filling the space. She stared at Ms. Chandler, still sleeping, and slightly resented how beautiful she looked, even under the florescent hospital lights. Life must be so easy for her, Sam thought.

Daisy had to be dead, Sam told herself. Where else could she be? Sure the police were looking, but after what she found in the attic, there was no hope left in her heart. She was sure Detective Brody found her mother's secrets as well, and would figure there was no use looking any further.

Sam shot up and almost jumped out of the bed as she remembered.

"What is it, Sam?" asked Carly as she was jolted from her sleep.

"The card! There was an adoption agency card in my mother's room! Oh my god, how could I have forgotten that! The attic made me forget!"

Carly was confused. "Sam, slow down."

"I have to talk to Detective Brody, right now!"

Sam voice was peppered with urgency and desperation, along with pain as her sudden movements disturbed her broken bones.

"He is coming to my house to check on you later this afternoon, once you are settled-in a bit. "But," Carly added in reaction to the panic on Sam's face, "we will call him when we're on our way, so that he can meet us there. Okay?"

"I just want to get out of here," said Sam. "Please, get me out of here."

CHAPTER 24

Carly was consumed with her thoughts during the silent drive from the hospital to her home. She was grateful the hospital staff was quick with Sam's discharge paperwork, and even more grateful for her friend, Todd. While she stayed at Sam's bedside all night, he worked on their spare bedroom, getting it prepared to receive its new owner.

He bought new sheets, rich and soft with an 800-thread count, along with new pillows and a fluffy blue and white comforter, which reminded him of a dream filled summer sky. He hoped Carly approved, and that Sam would feel warm and welcomed into her new space. He picked up a few magazines geared toward the young girl emerging into womanhood, along with books filled with teen angst and romance, and a new laptop, which he set up on her bedside table. At Carly's request, he also purchased girly smelling lotions, a new hair and toothbrush, and several fruit-flavored lip-glosses. He displayed them invitingly on top of the mirrored vanity, which sat adjacent to her bed.

CPS had brought over some of Sam's clothes from her room, which Todd washed and put away in the dresser drawers. Carly wanted to take Sam shopping for a new wardrobe, once Sam was feeling up to it.

As they pulled up to the house, Sam could not believe she was here. Ms. Chandler's lawn was a deep emerald green, and her shrubs were manicured perfectly. The winding walkway that led from the sidewalk to her front door was lined with red and white tulips, and there was a quaint bench that sat on her front porch with the inscription "May Your Time in Our Home Be Blessed" carved into the ornate backrest.

Todd and his white Yorkshire pup named Hope greeted them at the front door.

"Please come see your new home, Sam. This is my friend, Todd."

"So nice to meet you, Sam. I've heard so many wonderful things about you."

Sam looked at Ms. Chandler with confusion as she walked in the front door.

Once inside the foyer of the enormous home, Sam stared in disbelief. To her right was a winding staircase leading to the second floor. Straight ahead was the sitting room with beautiful burgundy furniture, a natural fireplace below an antique framed mirror that encompassed almost the entire wall, and high vaulted ceilings that compelled Sam to enter into the room's peaceful beauty.

Sam walked around the room, feeling as if she were in a different world as her bare feet sunk into the thick rug that sat atop the deep cherry wood floor, and stared at the art that adorned the creamy yellow walls. She was quite taken with one, a masterpiece depicting the back of a naked woman, outlined with thick black brush strokes, sitting upright while embracing one of her knees in an almost fetal position as she wept. The blue texture of the artwork told the sad tale of this woman and her excruciating grief. Sam began to cry, as she stood mesmerized by the painting. She knew this woman's pain. She, too, was condemned to a lifelong sentence of never ending shame and sorrow.

"That is a reproduction of the Pablo Picasso, Blue Nude," said Carly as she walked

behind Sam and rested her hand on her upper
back.

"It's beautiful," said Sam, as she wiped
back a tear.

"Detective Brody should be here any
minute. Why don't I show you your new room
while we wait."

As Carly led Sam through the spacious
kitchen, she pointed out the food pantry, the
cabinet full of dishes, where to find the silverware,
and then showed her the contents of the fridge.

"Help yourself to anything you like, at
anytime, Okay?"

"Okay," Sam replied.

Through the kitchen was another staircase
that led up to the long hallway of the upper floor,
which ended on the other side of the house.

"We have a double stairway up here. So
when you come home from school you can dash
right up at the front door, or, if you're hungry for
a midnight snack, you can take the opposite stairs
that will lead you right into the kitchen," Carly
said with a smile as they headed up to the
bedrooms.

"Neat."

One side of the hallway was lined with
four doors, while the other side was home to a
rich cherry wood banister with carved spindles

lined down the length of the floor. The house from this upper view was rather breath taking. Sam felt like she was in one of her stories, but would not admit so out loud. She kept her hardened exterior intact, she could not be happy without Daisy here to enjoy the surroundings as well.

"This is my bedroom," said Carly as she pointed into the first door, closest to the kitchen stairs. "The door is always open, no matter what time. Just let me know what you need. And here is the bathroom—Todd and I have our own bathrooms connected to our rooms, so you get this one all to yourself. That last door at the end of the hall is Todd's room, and this here is your new place to call home," Carly said with a smile as she opened the bedroom door.

Sam stepped inside in utter amazement. The room was the nicest room she had ever even dreamed about, let alone imagined she would ever sleep in. For a brief moment she softened as she brushed her hand along the new comforter.

"It looks like the sky," Sam said quietly as tears welled up in her eyes.

"Is it okay? We can pick out something different if you like," said Carly with concern.

"No, I love it. It's perfect. Daisy and I like to lie in the grass to look up on days when the clouds are really puffy, and we make up stories about the shapes the clouds make as they move across the sky. This bed reminds me of that," Sam whispered out, as Carly embraced her, and accepted her tears.

When Sam released herself from their embrace, Carly showed her around the rest of the room.

"The walls are pretty bare, but I thought we could go together and pick out things you like, so the room will feel like it really belongs to you."

Sam was about to object when the doorbell rang.

"That must be Brody," Carly began to say, but Sam was already heading out of the room and toward the stairs. Carly followed, with Hope excitedly yelping close behind.

"Good morning, Detective Brody. Please come in."

Sam felt such a rush of emotion that she charged toward Brody, and wrapped her one good arm around his waist as he entered through the front door.

He bent down to return her embrace and said, "Hey girl. You really gave me a scare yesterday."

"I need to tell you about what I found yesterday. About where Daisy might be," exclaimed Sam as they walked toward the sitting room.

Todd came walking out of the kitchen, "fresh coffee is brewing as we speak," he said.

"Detective Brody, this is my friend, Todd."

The men exchanged pleasantries as they all made them selves comfortable on the leather furniture. Brody felt his heart slightly deflate, as he was not expecting to find Carly living with a man. He wondered what she meant by friend, and then shook the question out of his head as he cleared his throat. He had no time for the daydreams of Carly, which occupied his thoughts lately.

Getting frustrated that she seemed to be the only one with any sense of urgency, Sam said, "Please, I might know where Daisy is. I think my mom gave her up for adoption. If we can just go back to my house I can show you..."

"We know Sam. We found the agency information when we searched your home last night."

"So there's a chance right? A chance that Daisy is still alive," she said, her voice pleading with him to agree with her.

"Of course," said Brody. "I am going to work around the clock until I find your sister, okay? What I need you to do, to help me, is stay here with Ms. Chandler and try to relax. I will concentrate much better knowing you are resting and healing. You're safe now, Sam. Trust me to bring Daisy home safe, too."

Sam nodded her head in agreement before releasing her relief, her small glimpse of possibility, into her knees as she bent over and let her sobs roll out.

CHAPTER 25

Daisy woke up from the jerky tremors of her body. She was so cold that her feet and hands ached, and shivers made their way down her spine, over and over again, making her body spasm continuously. She had curled herself into the tightest little ball on the floor, but her body offered no heat to give her even the smallest of comfort.

She painfully crawled to her red bag once she realized that she was lying in a puddle of her own urine. She found new shorts crumpled inside the bag and put them on, then took out a pair of faded blue leggings, and wrapped them around her icy feet. She wished she had brought warmer clothes. Sam would have packed what she needed, Daisy thought, if only she had been home. She took out a t-shirt and draped it over her arms as she curled into a ball once more.

Daisy had no concept of day or night, space or time. She yearned for Sam, for her voice, and for her sweet stories and warm bed. But most of all she ached for a hug, needed to feel the warmth of Sam's breath as she squeezed her tight and said what a good girl she was. She needed her dolly, needed to hug her tight, because surely dolly must be as cold as she was, but her body had gone stiff from the cold cement and she could no longer move her limbs to go and find her.

———————◆———————

"This isn't right, Terry. She's still a baby. We've never taken in such a young child, and we are playing with fire. It just doesn't feel right."

"What did you just say? Said Terry, as he threw his coffee mug across kitchen, shattering it against the wall, and smacked her across the face. "Since when did you start having an opinion in that small brain of yours? You only need to worry about what I tell you to do. Keep your mouth shut and your legs open, love. Leave the thinking to me."

The blow to Angel's cheek didn't even faze her. "I'm just nervous, baby. The investigation and search for Daisy is still headlining all the news channels. The police take a missing three-year-old much more serious than a missing run-away. I was just thinking that they aren't going to give up; the community won't let them. Forgive me, I just started to panic. I had no right to question you."

"Do you think I'm stupid, that I'm as ignorant as you? Do you think I've not thought that far ahead?"

"Of course not," quivered Angel. "I shouldn't have said anything. I trust you, baby, you know that."

"Now that's more like it, my Angel," said Terry as he walked over and kissed her forehead. "You just sit tight and keep quiet. And don't go talking to that baby down there, like you did that girl in Texas. Remember that? When you almost got us thrown in jail? You think it's easy to pack up and move, to get hired again in a new city, to have to explain my work history and why I've moved over and over again?"

Angel sat still. She knew that however she responded to Terry's questions could set him off into full-blown attack mode. So she instead purred up at him through her eyes, and smiled seductively, hoping the only thing he could see on her face was the adoration and obedience her master demanded.

"Don't be stupid again," Terry continued. "We're on our way to the ultimate payday. Soon I will never have to work again, although being so well connected certainly has its benefits."

Angel kept swallowing down the vomit that threatened to burst out and reveal her true feelings. "I can't wait for that day, baby. You always come through for us. Do you have anybody interested in her yet?"

She kept a smile on her face and her breathing even, as she hoped Terry would give her more information. She knew he was up to something because the children never stayed with them for this long without a plan in place. But so far, nobody had come calling, nor had they left the state to meet interested buyers. Something was different and she found herself terrified for the little girl lying on the cellar floor, right beneath the kitchen and right below Angel's cowardly feet.

"Oh, I have plans alright," said Terry with a dreamy glint in his snake-like eyes and a wicked grin on his bony face. "We just have to be patient while I obtain the necessary paperwork," he said, as he brushed back his jet-black hair, which had fallen out of place during his tantrum.

"Oh?" said Angel, matching his wicked grin while hiding the panic in her heart. "What kind of paperwork?"

"Let's just say, what we have been doing these past 10 years will seem like pocket change compared to how much that little girl will earn for me. I will make more money in just six months with her in Thailand, than I've made altogether since I started this business.

Angel nodded in agreement, but her expression gave away her complete confusion.

"Rich men vacation there solely for its reputation of young girls for sale, and will pay quadruple the norm for just ten minutes with that innocent porcelain skin of our very young, very special girl down there," Terry explained, as he pointed his finger to the cellar below.

Angel smiled, "We can retire by the Ocean like we've always dreamed of."

"Patience, my girl. Patience. If this goes well, we're in a new business. Why stop with this girl when there is so much money waiting for me to make? And do you know the most beautiful part of it all? When I return to the States, I simply leave the girl and the evidence behind. See how lucky you are to have me? You would be stupid and poor your whole life without me;

you'd still be that nothing that I plucked from the gutter."

Angel remembered all right. She also remembered the first time he beat her up, the first time he forced her into kidnapping a child, and the first time she tried to leave him. That first time was also her last, as she almost lost her life to Terry's rage. She was stuck with him for the rest of her life, and she was okay with that, but she could hardly bare the role she was playing in the lives of so many helpless victims.

When Angel first saw Terry on her routine corner on Hollywood Boulevard, she thought she had hit the jackpot. He smiled at her through the window of his shiny black corvette that perfectly matched his greased-back, jet-black hair. He slowed down and summoned Angel over to his car. He picked her, out of all the woman working that night, which both flattered and made Angel uneasy at the same time, as she always thought herself unworthy of anything good. And in Angel's world, a shiny new Corvette was certainly as good as it got.

There was something about Terry that immediately made her uneasy, but Angel was in no position to turn down a paying customer. She pushed her anxiety deep down and got into his car. She panicked when she saw a police badge on the belt of his pinstriped slacks, and demanded to be let out of the car. He laughed.

"This isn't a sting operation, love. I just couldn't pass up that blond hair and tight little ass of yours," he said as he gripped his fingers into her upper thigh.

Terry was nice to her at first. After their first encounter together, he told her she was the best sex he had ever had, and he began to meet regularly on her corner every Saturday night. It wasn't long before she fell in love with him, and without ever knowing what real love was, she thought his increasing control over her meant that he loved her, too.

She moved into his apartment not long after they met, and she thanked God daily for bringing a real man into her life to save her from the brutality of the streets. Even when Terry hit her, she knew that she deserved it. At least when she was beat up now, it came from the hands a hard working, successful man that really loved her, unlike her father whom she ran away from one hot summer night. She had decided at sixteen years old after her father, heavy with the stench of sweat and cheap whiskey, pealed his fat hairy body from the top of hers for the last time, that she might as well be paid for what the men in her life so often took. She packed her bags, snuck out of her window, and never looked back.

The clip of Terry holstering his gun snapped Angel back into the present. He secured his badge to his belt and put on his suit jacket, as he looked at her suspiciously.

"I'm off to work, make sure you give the girl water and something to eat. We don't want her dying down there, that'd be a fucking waste."

"You got it, Detective Jackson," said Angel, as she rose from her chair to plant a kiss on his cheek. Have a great day, baby."

As Terry walked out the front door, Angel stood alone in the kitchen, her body shaking while she wept into the palms of her hands. She was completely terrified at the new depth of Terry's ever growing darkness, was terrified that his need for torture seemed to intensify with each new captive they took, and was terrified, most of all, by her complete inability to stop the monster that ruled over her entire existence.

CHAPTER 26

Though Jackson would not admit so, he was growing anxious about how much his partner knew. He had covered his tracks with the cell phone, so there was no way that prepaid number could be traced back to him. And just for good measure, he had Angel wear a black wig and sunglasses when she purchased the phone from the Shop-Mart two counties away.

The website on the card was also untraceable to him, just a static site set up by colleagues of his from across the country. There was no information of value on there anyway, just an attempt to make the agency feel credible to the mothers willing to sell off their unwanted children.

By the time Jackson pulled into the station for their debriefing meeting, he had regained his arrogant confidence, knowing he could outsmart everyone, especially his know-it-all partner. The federal agents threw him off his game yesterday, but they, too, were beneath his intellect. He would manipulate the investigation to point towards Daisy's death, and discredit every other angle that popped up along the way. The town would soon forget, the media would move on to the next big story, and the case would go cold long before he retuned to the United States.

He was pleased at his stroke of luck in choosing Beth. Terry could tell she was just the woman he was looking for when he sat down in her section of the diner for the first time. After a few weeks of flirting with her as she checked in on his table and refilled his coffee, Beth opened up more and more about the burden of her children, of how ungrateful, and worse, disrespectful they were. Of how if she could do it all over again, she would have aborted them, rid herself of them before they sucked her, and everything she loved, completely dry.

Finally one afternoon during Terry's lunch, Beth asked him, "So what do you do, anyway?"

"Actually, I am glad you asked," said Terry with a smile. "I am the president of an adoption agency that I founded several years ago, after meeting a woman much like you."

Beth blushed as she calculated everything she had said about her children, and how to spin her words to keep this man interested in her.

Seeing Beth feeling befuddled he said, "I think we can both help each other out, Beth. Sit down, I have something I want to propose to you."

Once Jackson discovered Beth's, or rather Arlene's, past as he was doing the detective work required of him on Daisy's case, he quite literally laughed out loud. With her already under investigation for one murdered child, framing her for Daisy's murder was almost too easy. Soon he would live the life he was meant to, while Beth spent the rest of hers in jail.

"Good, you're here Detective Jackson," said Agent Townsend. "Lets get started."

"The dress recovered from the Beckett residence yesterday has been sent to the lab for DNA analysis. We are confident it will match the DNA in the underwear found with Jennifer Beckensworth's remains, which were also sent to the lab," said Townsend.

"We hope to find blood DNA matching Arlene Beckensworth mixed with Jennifer's blood on the dress. That will be the final evidence we need to obtain her arrest warrant," continued Agent Cooper.

"More pressing, however, is finding the whereabouts of Daisy," said Townsend. "Since this involves the open case our office has on Arlene, we have been instructed to aid in this investigation as well. I trust everyone here is on board with that, and that we will work together cohesively."

"Absolutely," said both Jackson and Brody in unison.

Brody looked at Jackson with suspicion. He had never known Jackson to be agreeable to outsiders treading on their territory in the entire year they had been partners. He was often uncooperative and obtuse with anyone, badge or not, offering to help or exchange information in regards to his case. His bull-headed arrogance often frustrated Brody. He could not put his finger on exactly why, but he had never fully trusted Jackson, and since Daisy's file landed in their hands, he had felt an unease that he couldn't explain.

Brody knew very little about Terry Jackson's past, other than he had worked for more departments in more cities than seemed reasonable. He often wondered what kept Jackson on the move, and his gut demanded he dig a little deeper into what his partner was hiding.

"Brody," said Jackson. "Townsend just asked you a question."

"What? Oh, sorry. Thinking about a tip I need to follow up on...

"No problem. What did you find out about the phone number on the card?"

"It belongs to a throw away phone, as we suspected it would be. It was assigned to Celebrate Mobile, a prepaid wireless phone company sold at almost every convenient store and gas station in the Midwest. We are tracking the sales of these phones in the past three months, within a 100 mile radius, although I am afraid the sales numbers will be overwhelming."

"Well that is a good start. Something just might stand out," replied Cooper.

"How about the mother's call history?" said Townsend.

"The phone company faxed me her history this morning," Brody replied, "and surprise, surprise. That was the last number dialed from Arlene's phone on the last day Daisy was seen. There was no other activity on her phone for three hours, until she called 911 that same afternoon to report Daisy missing."

Stupid woman, thought Jackson. He was tired of dealing with brainless ass women. How hard is it to cover up your tracks, he screamed to himself, lost inside his own head.

"Well, that is something," said Jackson as he joined back into the conversation. "I don't know if it's smart we spend all of our resources tracking down this child trafficking ring that may, or may not exist. We cannot assume the information on the card is connected at all with the phone number written on the back. Arlene could have written down the number to just about anybody on that card. A boyfriend, a teacher, anybody. And further still, both the phone number, as well as the agency information, may have nothing to do with Daisy's whereabouts whatsoever."

Jackson could tell the rest of the men were not buying it.

"All I'm saying, is that just because she wrote down a number on the back of that card, does not mean the two pieces of information are connected to one another. Maybe the card was the only thing in her purse to write on. Or maybe the card was given to her to jot the number down on. Maybe the actual phone number in question was to a married lover of Arlene's who got the phone to hide his indiscretions. We just don't know at this point, and we can't be too narrow in our thinking. It will be detrimental to the case if we have tunnel vision down one, murky at best, possibility."

"I agree, Detective Jackson," said Townsend. "But with all do respect, this is the best lead we have and to not give it the urgency and due diligence it demands, would be nothing short of negligent."

"Oh I totally agree, Agent. All I'm pointing out, is this may not be our answer. My gut, and it has never steered me wrong, is telling me Daisy is already gone. Even though Arlene dialed that number on that day, the call could be sheer coincidence. Without all of the facts, concentrating on that phone call may be steering our investigation in the wrong direction. It is also negligent, with all due respect to you, too, sir, if we do not take into account Arlene's past, if we do not take into account what the end result of her last missing child turned out to be. That is all I am saying," said Jackson, with his voice calm and full of authority.

The uneasy feeling in the pit of Brody's stomach intensified. Although this was the agitation he had come to expect from his partner, there was more of an edge to his irritation than normal. Brody would tread lightly from now on, and hold his cards a little closer to his chest.

"Of course, Detective. Nobody is suggesting this case is anywhere near solved," said Townsend, as he tried to dissolve the tension that filled the room. "You are correct, the adoption agency may not be our answer, but I hope to God that it is, as the alternative leaves us with virtually no hope to find Daisy alive."

All four men shook their heads in joint agreement.

"Agent Cooper and I are going to interview Arlene where she is being held, and confront her with the new evidence found in her home and its connection with Jennifer's murder. Hopefully, she will give in to defeat and confess. And just maybe she will help lead us to Daisy as well. But knowing Arlene, I'm afraid she would rather die with the satisfaction of keeping her secrets, than make a plea deal to aid in Daisy's return home."

Jackson silently prayed that was true as he got up from the conference table and headed towards the Lieutenant's office.

"Where are you going?" asked Brody.

"I just need to talk to the Lieutenant for a minute."

"About what?"

"I need to answer to you, and those FBI monkeys now?" Jackson shot back, before he collected himself and calmed his temper. "Oh, you know I'm just kidding, Brody. Just trying to get you riled up. I was actually going to talk to you about it, too. I need to take a leave of absence. Not too long, six months tops."

"A leave of absence?" asked Brody. "When?"

"Right away, I'm afraid. As early as next week, actually."

"What? Why? We are right in the middle of this investigation and you have to take leave?"

"My wife is terminally ill with cancer, and her doctors here have no treatment options left to offer us," replied Jackson, his voice dripping with indignation. "Our only hope is a controversial new treatment only offered overseas."

"You're married?" exclaimed Brody, suddenly acutely aware of just how little he knew about this man.

"Jesus Christ, Brody. A little sensitivity would be nice," yelled Jackson, as he headed into the lieutenant's office and shut the door behind him.

The sweat showing through Jackson's suit coat, and the throbbing vein on his forehead, gave away the emotion raging under Jackson steady voice and stoic demeanor during most of their meeting. And now this.

"Just what are you hiding, Jackson," Brody whispered to himself before heading out of the station.

CHAPTER 27

Angel prepared scrambled eggs with melted cheddar cheese to take down to Daisy for breakfast. She must be truly starving, and even though the smell of the cooking eggs made Angel's already weak stomach churn, she prepared them anyway, knowing Daisy needed more than bread and water to keep her healthy.

She filled a glass with orange juice, and then balanced the plate in the crook of her arm as she pulled the light switch with the other. She looked down the dusty steps to the tiny lump lying below. Even with the sudden burst of light filling the cellar, Daisy did not move.

"Daisy," Angel called out as she headed down the steps, each one creaking ominously under her weight.

She remained absolutely still.

Maybe she is just sleeping, Angel hoped, as adrenaline began to rush through her veins.

"Daisy, I brought you some breakfast," she said as she set the dishes on the bottom step. She moved closer and knelt down beside the little girl. She rested her hand on Daisy's small diaphragm, and then breathed out in relief as she felt Daisy's stomach rise and fall. She was indeed breathing, but her breaths seemed too shallow, and her skin was ice cold.

"Daisy, I need you to wake up. I need you to wake up right now."

Following her instinct, Angel scooped up the little girl and held her close to her own body for warmth, but it took her only seconds to know that Daisy needed much more heat than her own body could offer. She had to warm this little girl up, and now. She rushed Daisy up the stairs and into the bathroom to run a warm bath. Daisy was still unconscious, so she kept the water shallow and lowered her inside slowly, clothes and all. She took a washcloth and used it to transfer the warm water over Daisy's chest and head.

Daisy started to squirm a bit as the temperature of her skin began to slowly warm up. Angel ran to the bedroom and grabbed a dark red, wool blanket from the cedar chest that sat at the foot of Terry's bed. Everything in the house was Terry's and Terry's only, and he was sure to tell Angel that every single day.

She trembled at the thought of what Terry would do if he found out she did this, if he found out she brought this girl upstairs. But she couldn't just walk away when the girl seemed to be facing certain death. Terry wouldn't like that either, would he?" she reasoned with herself. He had charged her with keeping the girl alive, that is what he had said before he left for work, she told herself again. She would be able to talk her way out of her insubordination, if it came to that, she prayed silently to herself, over and over again.

Angel picked the limp body up and out of the water, a body now shivering and trembling with a chill that reached deep into every tissue in her tiny body. She wrapped Daisy up in the warmth of the wool and carried her to the living room couch. She sat with Daisy in her lap and wrapped her arms around the red cocoon to share as much extra warmth as her own body would provide.

Daisy opened her eyes and blinked herself back into consciousness with confusion and unease.

"Hi there, Daisy. You gave me a little scare just now," said Angel.

"Sorry, ma'am."

"Don't be sorry, little lady. It wasn't your fault. We let you get too cold down there. I didn't realize you were so cold."

"I was a good girl, though," Daisy beamed up at her, even under the exhaustion of her chill. I wanted to scream and cry but I listened to Uncle Terry and kept real, real quiet."

Angel felt her heart crack open and bleed as she looked down into this sweet girl's eyes. I am so stupid, Angel said to herself, I did it again. This is exactly why she had closed herself off, had allowed herself zero contact with the children they had taken into their ring in the years following their flee from Texas. Angel promised herself she would never get emotionally attached again. Because of her selfish stupidity, and her role in the Texas Teen's escape attempt, that girl paid the ultimate price for her mistakes, and Angel was beaten dangerously close to that very same fate.

Terry promised the next time she became too involved, he really would kill her. And Beth knew that to be true with all of her heart.

"Are you ok, ma'am?" said Daisy as she looked up into Angel's face and saw a single tear sliding down.

"I am just fine. How are you? Are you warming up yet?"

"Yes, ma'am. I am just feeling hungry."

"Of course you are. I have your breakfast downstairs waiting for you," Angel said as she moved Daisy off of her lap and onto the couch. "I am going to get you a pair of my socks to keep your feet warm down there."

When Angel returned from the bedroom, Daisy was crying into her knees as her legs were curled up into her chest.

"I don't want to go back into the basement," she choked out through her tears. "I want to stay up here with you."

"You don't understand what you are saying, Daisy. That is not possible. Uncle Terry will be very, very angry if he comes home and sees you up here. We need to keep him calm, don't we? This needs to stay our little secret, do you understand?"

Daisy imagined Uncle Terry's cold eyes and scary laugh, and shook her head in absolute agreement.

CHAPTER 28

S am woke up in her new surroundings after a long night of tossing and turning. Her endless thoughts kept her mind racing, and her heart thudded too loudly in her chest to allow sleep to settle in. The sun rising through the bedroom window was the last thing Sam remembered before exhaustion won over her tired mind.

She sat up in her bed and wondered what time it was. Her pain medication had worn off sometime during the night, and the left side of her body, from her arm down to her pelvic bone, throbbed intensely. She carefully swung her legs off the side of the bed and headed down to the kitchen.

"Good morning, Sam" exclaimed Carly with a voice full of pure sunshine.

"Good morning," Sam winced out in return.

"Oh, you poor thing. Sit down here at the table while I get your medication."

Carly grabbed a cold water bottle from the massive double door, stainless steel refrigerator and brought it to Sam, along with her morning dose of pills to help manage her pain as her injuries healed.

"What can I make you for breakfast, dear? Well, actually it is almost lunch time, now."

"Lunch time?" asked Sam, with an edge of anxiety. "I'm sorry, I didn't mean to sleep so long. I am really sorry."

"Don't be sorry, Sam. You need your sleep. I want you to sleep as much as your body needs, okay? You don't ever have to be sorry here, this is your house now, too. So you sleep as you like, and eat as you like, whenever you like. I mean it," said Carly. "I hope you learn to trust in that."

"Yes, ma'am."

"And no ma'am stuff, either. You can call me Carly, if you are comfortable with that," she said with a smile.

"Okay," Sam replied with hesitation.

"Today is our first Sunday Fun-day! Todd and Hope will be away for the week visiting his parents, so it's just you and me, and we can do absolutely anything you like. Your cast will limit us for a while, so no putt-putt golfing or horseback riding for us just yet," Carly said with a light-hearted laugh. "Do you have anything in mind?"

Sam just stared back in return. She could not form a response in her mind, let alone say anything out loud.

"Well I was thinking, if you are up for it, we can go shopping for your room like I mentioned yesterday. I really want you to feel at home here."

"What more could the room need?" Sam asked. "It already has everything."

"Well we can just go to the department store and look around. I was thinking since you like the art in the sitting room so much, that we could look at pieces to put up in your room, too. Also, you're going to need more sheets, a bedside lamp, and anything else that might strike your fancy." Why don't you go up and shower while I fix you something to eat. I make a mean grilled turkey and cheese sandwich on garlic bread. Does that sound okay?"

"Yes, ma'am, err, Carly. That sounds great, it really does. But if it isn't too much trouble, do you think we can go to the eye doctor instead? I can hardly see through my glasses anymore and my mom never has the time, or the money to buy me a new pair. I won't pick out anything expensive though, I promise. Just the cheapest frames they have will be fine for me." Sam waited for Carly's response with her head down, immediately feeling ashamed and embarrassed that she had asked.

Carly's heart dropped with sadness from the expression on Sam's face. "Oh, Sam. Listen to me sweetheart. You are one of the most beautiful girls I have ever known, with a heart and soul full of love. You are worthy of everything, big or small, that your heart desires, worthy of everything you can dream of. Do you understand what I'm saying?"

Sam didn't understand, though. She could not yet understand how unique and inspiring she truly was, and how all of her qualities, the very essence of Sam's being, was a gift to the world not often found together in one pre-teen package.

"Of course we can go pick out new glasses for you, as long as I can help you choose the perfect pair," Carly continued. "Have you ever thought about trying contacts? You have such beautiful eyes."

"Not really," replied Sam. "Well, actually I have, but it was never worth asking for. My mother would have never spent her money on something like that for me."

"Well you are with me now, kid," said Carly, with a smile full of honest anticipation. "We have two whole weeks off from school, that's plenty of time to shop 'till our hearts' content. Now go head upstairs and enjoy yourself a nice long shower. There's a closet inside the upstairs bathroom, and you'll find everything you need, including the waterproof sleeve for your cast."

At that, Sam stood up from the table and climbed the long staircase to the bathroom and shut the door behind her. She opened the long white pine door to the closet and stared in disbelief. There were stacks and stacks of towels, plush and inviting, and so clean. She picked one up from atop the stack, colored a warm olive green, and held it to her nose as she inhaled the crisp clean fragrance. How did Ms. Chandler get her towels smelling so wonderful, she wondered, as no matter how many times Sam washed her towels at home they still stunk of mold and dirty water.

She placed the towel gingerly on the granite-topped vanity before investigating the closet further. There were six different scented body wash options to choose from, as well as at least a dozen mesh washcloths sitting next to them. She smelled each of them before deciding on her favorite, labeled Paradise Dream. The scent was potent with a mix of coconut and avocado oil which reminded Sam of one of her far away stories, Daisy's favorite, which ended with the two girls playing carefree on a beach under a sun filled sky.

Sam let the hot water beat down on her body for what seemed like an eternity. She had never experienced such powerful water pressure, which made her grateful beyond expression. She began to cry as she imagined the water beating off the years of built up filth that covered her skin. She washed herself, over and over, until her body was bright red from the water's heat and her feverish scrubbing.

She stepped out of the bathtub and dried herself before wrapping the towel around her rejuvenated body. She took a new toothbrush and tube of toothpaste out of the closet and brushed her teeth with vigor.

Once she cleaned up the bathroom, and put away everything as she had found it, she quickly scampered to her room, hoping Ms. Chandler would not see her in nothing but a towel. Once inside, she shut the bedroom door and sat down at her vanity. After putting her glasses on she stared at her reflection in the mirror. All she could think about was Daisy, and she hoped that wherever she was, the home was as nice as this, and she prayed that her sweet baby was being taken care of.

After she got herself dressed, which was a lot harder than she had anticipated with her casted arm, she returned to the vanity once more. She stared at the lip-gloss tubes that sat on top, before picking one up and applying it to her supple lips. She looked at herself in the mirror before quickly wiping the tint from her mouth, embarrassed for hoping it would actually look good.

As she silently walked down the steps, she had gotten really good at being silent over the years, she overheard Ms. Chandler on the phone.

"Of course, Detective. I'm glad you caught us because we were heading out in a few. Absolutely, I will let Sam know you are coming. See you soon," she said before setting her phone down on the kitchen table.

"Was that Detective Brody?" asked Sam as she entered the room.

"Yes it was. He is on his way over; he said he has a few more questions for you. Are you feeling up to that?"

"Sure," said Sam. She kept her tone flat, even though happy butterflies danced in her stomach. She wasn't sure if they were from possible news of her Daisy, or from the anticipation of seeing Brody again. Probably both, she decided, though she didn't really understand why she liked the Detective so much.

"Good," said Carly, as she tried to hide her own butterflies and beating heart. She was very much looking forward to Brody's visit as well, she realized.

"Eat up while it's hot. I'm going to freshen up a bit."

Sam sat down at the table and watched Carly as she jogged up the steps, and wondered why such a beautiful woman wasn't married with kids of her own. Sam shifted her attention back to her famished stomach and took a bite of her sandwich, delicately prepared with a blend of fine melted cheeses and fresh garlic, which enhanced the smoky flavor of the fresh turkey breast that rested warmly in between the thick slices of grilled bread. Sam's jaw stung from the delicious intensity of that first bite, and she was sure she had never tasted anything so amazing in all her life.

She gobbled up her meal, grateful that Ms. Chandler was not around to see her poor manners, as she felt like a stray dog scarfing its food to satisfy the demanding growl of its empty belly. Just as she drank the last sip of her kiwi mango juice blend, she heard the doorbell ring. She jumped up from the table as Carly came rushing down the other side of the staircase. As Sam rounded the corner to the foyer, she saw Ms. Chandler standing still in front of the door while smoothing out her floral sundress and taking a few deep breaths.

Carly opened the door and the bright cheer glowing from her smile evaporated instantly as her eyes locked with a cold stare from a scrawny man with a sharp face, his expression as hard as his slicked back hair. She recognized him as Detective Brody's partner from her meeting with them in her principal's office. Just as she opened the screen door to welcome the Detective in, she saw Brody round the corner and head up her walk. Carly sighed in relief as she watched his strong legs head toward her front door.

"Good afternoon, Detectives. Please come in."

"Thank you, ma'am," said Brody in return, as he respectfully nodded his head toward her before crossing the threshold into her cheerful home. "You remember my partner, Detective Jackson?"

"Of course, so nice to see you again," returned Carly, as she held out her hand to Jackson's and accepted his handshake. His palms were cold and wet, and curiously hard—as if she were shaking pure bone with just enough thin, taut skin to cover through to his fingertips.

"Hey there, Sam! How are you feeling?" Brody asked, as he saw Sam standing alone in the distance.

"Much better, sir. Thank you."

Brody turned his attention back to Carly and saw her beaming with love as she looked over at Sam's sad face and sheepish posture. His pulse began to race as he witnessed the genuine goodness this woman possessed, and her heaven-like beauty played an equal role to the fondness and warmth that filled his chest, growing more intense each time he spoke with her.

"Have you eaten yet, Detectives? Can I get you anything?"

"A cup of coffee would be perfect, if it isn't too much trouble," Brody replied.

"No trouble at all. Follow me to the kitchen while I brew us a fresh pot." Carly wondered if caffeine was the wisest idea, with her nerves already jittering up and down and all around just having Brody so close to her again.

CHAPTER 29

Carly had never felt this way around anybody, had never felt the electricity that seemed to extend out from every cell in her body and reach into Brody's, before returning back to her with a jolting force that made speaking, even thinking, require every bit of concentration she could muster. So this is what they mean about chemistry, she thought. It was both exhausting and exhilarating, and something Carly wanted absolutely no part of.

"You look really great, Sam," said Brody as they sat down on either side of the kitchen table, Brody and Jackson on one side and Sam on the other. I can see already that Ms. Chandler is taking good care of you."

"Have you found anything new about Daisy?" was all Sam could reply.

"Not yet, sweetie. That is why I'm here, I need to ask you some more questions, tough questions, okay?"

"Okay," Sam answered, as her anxiety reverberated through her single word reply.

Carly turned from the counter, "Should I leave the room and give you privacy?"

"That's up to you and Sam. You're her legal guardian, therefore, privy to any information regarding our interview. He looked at Sam, "It's up to you, girl, would you rather we speak alone?"

"No, I don't mind if she stays." Carly's presence made Sam feel more at ease, but she was not yet willing to let down the fortress of brick that surrounded her fragile feelings and vulnerable heart.

"Good, I think that is best," said Brody as he shook his head in positive affirmation of Sam's response.

"I want to start with your day-to-day interactions with your mother. How did she treat you and Daisy?"

"Fine, I guess. It really depended on her mood."

"Was she violent with you? Did she ever hit you or your sister? Other than the time I witnessed the other day, that is."

Sam closed up immediately from living her entire life in fear, from years of lying about the beatings she could never escape, and from her constant embarrassment of fading bruises and smelly clothes.

"I want you to know you can trust me, Sam. And you can trust Ms. Chandler as well. We will be by your side every step of the way through this transition, through this investigation that, I know, must be like walking through your own personal hell every single minute of your day."

The room's tension lifted slightly as Sam's shoulders relaxed down from their stiff stance on either side of her taught spine and erect neck.

"Your mother is locked away, sweetie. We will never let her hurt you again." Brody would do everything in his power to keep that promise, even knowing how inept the family court system could sometimes be. He was motivated, now more than ever, to put the monster that had the audacity to call herself a mother behind bars so that she would never see the light of day as a free woman again. The more he learned about Arlene's past, and the depths of her inhumanity, the more he knew society was not safe with such evil lurking and hiding deceivingly in plain sight.

"But what if you are wrong? What if she does get out? You don't know her like I do, she always gets her way," Sam said, breaking Brody's concentrated trance.

"You will help me, Sam. Just tell me about her, about what she has done to you and Daisy. I need every detail you can manage right now, and if things were even half as bad as I have imagined them to be, you will never have to live a day in fear of your mother ever again. You have my word."

Carly came to the table with two ornate mugs filled with black coffee which deliciously contrasted against the off-white ceramic, with fresh steam billowing up around the wide, inviting rims. She served them to the men before she sat down at the table, in the chair closest to Sam, and rested her steady hand on top of Sam's trembling one.

An hour passed while Sam told the details of her mother's deranged attacks, the dangerous men that Arlene regularly brought in and out of the house, and how she was strong enough to handle the despair that hung heavy in every inch that composed the only home the sisters had ever known. Strong enough, that is, until Arlene began channeling her hatred into Daisy with more than just her damaging words.

"I got too good at staying out of my mom's way," said Sam. "I avoided every possible thing, every possible word that might set her off. I tried to teach Daisy, too, but she's just a baby. She didn't understand. So when my mom needed to explode, Daisy started becoming her new target."

"How long has she been physically abusive with Daisy?" Asked Brody.

"It started soon after last summer break was over, and I had to go back to school. My mom was so angry at Daisy for crying every morning when I tried to leave the house. It wasn't her fault she was crying, though. She was just used to me being home to keep her company all day long."

"So that is why you started skipping school," said Carly, as she squeezed Sam's hand with understanding.

"Yes, ma'am," said Sam as her cheeks flushed with embarrassment. "One morning Daisy had a really high fever and didn't want me to leave her side. I kept begging her to stay in bed and stop crying but she followed me to the front door anyway, sobbing and begging me not to leave her. I tried picking her up to calm her down, but I was too late. The noise had woken up my mom and she came charging out of her bedroom right toward us. I held Daisy tight and gripped her head against my chest, but she ripped Daisy out of my arms and threw her into the back of our living room couch. Daisy's back hit directly against the wood pole thing that stuck out, separating the two cushy sides, do you know what I mean?"

"Yes I do," said Brody. "It dug into my back when I sat down to speak to your mother that first time. I had to slide over a bit to get comfortable, I know exactly what you're talking about."

"Yeah. Anyway, Daisy started crying even harder from the pain so my mom forced Daisy's face up toward the ceiling by yanking the back of her hair, and threatened if she didn't shut up that second she was going to get it. She didn't even wait, though. She never does. While one had was still holding her hair, the other smacked Daisy as hard as she could across her cheek. I don't exactly know what happened next because my mom dragged Daisy by one leg to her room, and all I could hear was the smack of my mother's hand against Daisy's bare skin, until there was no more yelling, and no more crying. That was the first day I skipped school," Sam said to Carly, with apologetic eyes.

Brody struggled to keep his emotions level as he took his notes. "How often did your mother have these episodes with you and your sister?"

"I am not sure. Sometimes every day, other times we would go days without even seeing her."

"Did you ever hear your mom talk about saving money, or recently receiving a large sum of money, say from a boyfriend?"

"I never talked about money, ever. She said I was an ungrateful bi..," Sam trailed off, mortified with herself for swearing in front of grown-ups, let alone her teacher and two policemen.

"Ungrateful Bitch," Brody continued for her.

Sam nodded her head. "The only time I risked asking my mom for anything was when I was out of food to make for Daisy. And even then, I waited until I scraped up every bit of food left in the house—even if it was expired—before asking if I could walk to the grocery store."

"And would she give you money to do so?"

"Usually. She always slapped me across the face, or hit the back of my head first, but once she cooled down she would give me at least 20 bucks to get us some food. Sometimes I would have to spend half of that on her coffee and flavored creamer, but as long as I had a little bit of money, I could make do."

"Didn't your mom eat at home?" Asked Brody.

"Usually not. She works at a diner close to home, and she ate her meals there most of the time. She bragged to me one time about sleeping with the cook and how in love with her he was, so she ate for free whenever she wanted. Like I said before, she went out with all kinds of different men. They bought her dinner a lot."

"I know I have asked you this before, Sam. But did you notice any new male friends coming around before Daisy disappeared?"

"Not really, it had been a calm few weeks," said Sam, as she laughed for the first time in a long time at her witty response.

"That is all for now, hon. Thank you so much for speaking so openly with me. I will be in touch with you the moment I know something more."

Carly rose from her seat along with Brody and Jackson to see them out.

"Can I talk to you privately for a moment, Ms. Chandler?"

The two walked slowly toward the front door as Jackson took the empty cups to the kitchen sink, and Sam walked back up to her bedroom to be alone.

"I spoke with Sam's ER doctor this morning and he was quite alarmed. He found multiple concussions, in various stages of healing, during Sam's CT scan," said Brody.

"So I guess Sam wasn't making up her headaches just to get out of my class," Carly replied. I was hoping she was making them up, anyway. But I knew better."

"And you were right about her broken ribs, I'm afraid. The doctor saw fractures on the upper two ribs on her right side, that had healed themselves unevenly due to improper rest, and possible re-injury before they were fully healed."

"Good God," Carly choked out. And who knows what injuries she has suffered over the years that didn't show up. Why didn't the doctor tell me about this before we left the hospital?"

"Not sure, but I wanted to make you aware. She will need follow up visits to address the concussions, so make sure to make an appointment for her right away."

"Of course, Detective, and thank you." She reached out to shake Brody's hand and about fell to the floor once his skin met hers. His simple touch made her numb with instant yearning, and she wondered how her weakened legs held the weight of her vibrating body.

Brody slid into his car and slammed the door, then pounded the lock for good measure to trap himself safely inside as he waited for his partner. As Carly politely shook his hand in nothing more than a gesture of gratitude, he nearly grabbed ahold of her to pull her close into his body. He ached to feel the warmth of her heart against his own, and could barely concentrate on their conversation, as he could not look at her mouth without imagining what it would be like to kiss her perfect heart-shaped lips—how he craved for the love of a woman like Carly Chandler once more.

Brody needed silence to clear his head, and angrily shut the radio off after Jackson had tried to blast the heavy metal garbage he called music. He needed to get Carly out of his mind, needed to fight back against feelings he never wanted to deal with again. The aftermath of grief from losing such a love was more than he could bear a second time around.

"What I would do to that woman," said Jackson in his attempt at breaking the silence. "I would love to look down at those pretty little lips around me," he said with the most foul laugh and grotesque smile.

Brody slammed his brakes and turned sharply into the gas station to their right. He threw the car in park and flew out, opened the passenger side door with one hand as the other grabbed Jackson out by the neck of his tie.

Brody's massive body held Jackson's weak frame against the car with little effort.

"Don't you ever speak to me of Ms. Chandler, or any woman, as part of your vulgar fantasies again. Do you understand me?"

Brody's temper flared and his body shook as he fought back the urge to bloody Jackson's arrogant face and bullshit grin.

Brody released Jackson and took a few steps back. "I think it's best you get reassigned to a different, less labor intensive, case since you're leaving soon anyway."

Jackson smoothed his hair with both hands and adjusted his suit coat back into place. "Hit a hot button, there, did I? Don't worry, Brody," said Jackson as he slid back into the car. "Didn't know you had your own interest in Ms. Do-Good back there. I'll leave her all to you," he laughed as he shut the door.

Brody tried to even his breathing as he, too, got back into the car.

"Tell me again how your wife is dying of cancer? Lucky woman you have there," Brody spit out as he clicked in his seatbelt and screeched out of the parking lot.

CHAPTER 30

Angel quickly put a pair of socks, the thickest she could find, on Daisy's cold feet, and replaced her wet clothes with the warmest options she could find haphazardly packed in the bag downstairs, bundled her up again, and carried the sweet girl back down into the cellar. She walked slowly down each step, finding it difficult to keep her balance in the narrow space of the stairwell. Once they reached the bottom, she placed Daisy on the floor and made sure the red wool was as tight and secure around her body as it could be.

"Wait here, Daisy. I'm gonna warm these eggs up for you."

Angel quickly returned with the eggs, steaming as the fresh cheese melted into goo, along with a hot cup of tea to warm Daisy from the inside out.

Daisy struggled to loosen the grip of the blanket from around her neck by moving her shoulders back and forth underneath, then broke her arms free as she accepted the gift of food from her new savior.

As she ate, she looked up at Angel, sitting a few steps up from the ground. "What is your name? I don't remember."

"Angel," she replied.

"Are you a real Angel?" Asked Daisy, with childlike wonder.

"No honey, far from it," she answered back, her voice full of regret and self-loathing. "Drink your tea while it's hot."

Angel tried to turn her tone back into the harsh stone it had been ladled with before, but was unable to fully do so. She had to get away to think, to stop her heart from bleeding further for this little girl she was unable to help, and to figure out how to end her own life, as it was her only escape from this new depth of her living hell.

"Please don't leave me alone," said Daisy, as Angel began to ascend up the stairs.

"I have to, Daisy. I am not allowed to be down here and Terry could come home at any moment." She walked back down the steps, wrapped Daisy in the blanket once more, and gathered the empty dishes before running up the steps and swiftly shutting the door behind her. Angel had to escape Daisy's presence that instant, before she gave into the voice pleading in her head to flee far away with the little girl, and her perfect, squeaky voice.

Alone once again, Daisy sat in the silence and looked around. Angel had left the light on, but Daisy was becoming used to her dark dungeon and was not so scared of the curious noises and threatening concrete walls anymore.

She was beginning to sweat under the trapped heat of her wool enclosure, so she wiggled her way out and stood up to spread the blanket across the hard, unforgiving floor. She struggled as she tried her hardest to lay the blanket out evenly, but its weight and size were too much for her to manage. After a few tries of wafting the material in the air, hoping it would land against the ground straight and perfect, Daisy hopped her happy self to each corner of the red fabric, and straightened it out as best she could.

"How did you get way over there, Dolly?" Daisy asked out loud, as she spotted her baby lying in front of the rusted chains Terry had threatened her with the night before. She walked over and scooped Dolly up before scampering back to the safety her spot just in front of the steps seemed to offer.

"Look at what Ms. Angel gave us, Dolly! Isn't it soft and beautiful?" Daisy said, her voice almost songlike, as she stroked the softness of her new comfort. The first she had received since her arrival. "I promised things would be okay, didn't I," reassured Daisy, as she lay down with a full belly and a happier heart. Things might not be so bad until Sam finds me after all, thought Daisy, as she smiled at how proud Sam was going to be with her for staying brave and strong.

———————◆———————

Angel sat in Terry's office and stared at his computer screen, as the cursor throbbed back at her with impatience in the blank browser bar, waiting for her to hurry up and decide what she was looking for.

Her initial intention was to search for the easiest way to take her life, but the image of Daisy, the vision of her cold and almost lifeless body, would not stop playing in Angel's head, trapping her in an internal battle with no reasonable solution.

Her hands shook as she entered the words Children and Thailand into the search engine and waited for the results. As she scrolled through the links, she skimmed the information highlighted beneath each one before clicking and confirming how *unspeakable Daisy's fate truly was.*

"*Girls as young as 9, and sometimes younger, are enslaved into Thai brothels, which are composed from run down and dilapidated buildings that stand in rows along a dirt road, contrasting completely against the new Western-Style Mall built just a few streets away to cater to newly wealthy Thai men, and the sex bound Thailand tourists.*"

"*Brothels are ever seeking younger and younger prostitutes, to build its clientele and reputation for fresh girls.*"

"*Young girls new to their enslavement in these Thai brothels, are tortured, beaten, raped, and deprived of food, until they are fully indoctrinated.*"

"*Girls as young as four have been sold into enslavement, and are used mostly for imagery purposes. Further, they are forced into performing sexual acts on other girls for big paying clients, and in some cases, they are taught to perform oral sex, which they call "boom boom", until their bodies have grown enough to allow penetration.*"

"*Thailand prostitutes enter enslavement, most often, from being sold by their own parents to pimps who seek out the most destitute families in the poorest of villages, and promise to send large sums of money in return. Other times young girls are kidnapped by Thailand thugs, never to be seen by their families again. Undercover journalist, Michael K. Smith, reports that a new nightmare has begun to emerge in these brothel houses, in which sex trafficking rings from the US and other countries abroad are taking their slaves into the Thailand underworld, where brokers and brothel owners will pay a much higher sum to acquire American and European girls to bolster their status and attract higher paying customers. Brothel owners use the purchase of these foreign children to combat the rapid loss of their slaves due to HIV, and the need to pay off families for the daughters they were forced to sell."*

Angel could not read anymore. She closed the open browser windows, full of nightmarish greed and incomprehensible inhumanity, with deliberate and forceful clicks before clearing the Internet history to keep her curiosity hidden from Terry.

She fully realized as she paced back and forth around the office that her role in trafficking girls was no different than the vile pimps she had just read about. That she was just as vile a human being for gaining the trust of both runaway teenagers and desperate mothers looking for a way out of their hopeless existence. She had always rationalized her actions, had lied to herself until she believed that these girls may have a chance for a better life in the business, than from the nothingness they had come from.

Angel would always escape her guilt-filled compassion with pills and alcohol during the first few days of the girls captivity when Terry would beat them into submission, would spill his demons over their bodies, over and over, until they were fully broken and ready for work.

"I can't do this anymore," Angel cried out, as she fell to the floor in a heaving ball of sobbing desperation.

CHAPTER 31

A week had passed and Sam was feeling less and less pain as her fractured bones healed more quickly than she expected. She never believed, never dared to dream even, that she would experience such genuine care from an adult, such patience and understanding, and such lavish gifts she still thought she ought not accept.

Carly had kept her promise and Sam had a new pair of glasses, small silver frames that rested perfectly above her cheekbones, with detailed silver Daisies etched and carved into both sides of the frame's sturdy, silver arms. Carly had found them amongst the hundreds of choices that adorned the wall in the ophthalmologist's office, and brought them to Sam saying, "these are the ones". And of course she was right, and they were perfect. Sam left, however, glasses free as she tested out her new contacts lenses and felt, for the first time, somewhat normal.

The pair continued their week off school with a three day shopping spree, picking out an entirely new wardrobe, more clothes than Sam had ever owned in her entire life, combined. Carly didn't even mind when Sam stopped self-consciously at a freestanding display filled with fancy and expensive underwear. "These are perfect," she said, sparing Sam from her own awkwardness. Then, after much convincing, Sam was fitted for a bra, followed by Carly's insistence she get several options in all sorts of fun and different colors.

And then there was Sam's day in the hair salon, a day full of pampering, shampooing, cutting and styling; and teaching Sam how to utilize her gorgeous hair which now curled naturally around all the right places The hair stylist worked magic through her cutting shears, and turned a simple haircut into a true work of art. As Sam's chair swiveled back toward the mirror, it took several seconds before she could connect the image staring back to her as her own; was unable to believe how good, how normal, she looked. Sam's fragile soul was still too broken to recognize the beauty that reflected back at her, and that the adoring hairstylists had fallen in love with her self-conscious innocence.

"You look beautiful, Sam," Carly gushed, as she squeezed her arms around the back of Sam's shoulders. "Simply beautiful."

Now as Sam sat in her pajamas—actual pajamas and not her worn out t-shirt, which no longer offered any modesty as her legs grew lean and tall and her bottom began to round evenly with the new curve of her hips—she felt nervous about returning to school in the morning. Her mind never wandered far from her Daisy, though. Her worry and guilt of failing to protect her baby as she had promised was ever present, and the sturdy thread, which quilted each broken piece of her soul to Daisy's, continued to weave through Sam's every thought and action. And if Sam sat quietly enough, as she did in this moment, Daisy's presence billowed around her in the stillness, and spoke to her through the whispers of her pounding heart. In these moments Sam knew Daisy was still alive, and scared, and dangerously desperate for Sam's strength and reassurance.

Carly entered the room with her thoughtfully prepared back-to-school present, and saw Sam staring off somewhere far away. She was deep in thought as she sat with her legs crisscrossed atop her neatly made comforter, with her back leaning against the headboard for support. "Hi there, babe. I brought you something to celebrate your return to school," said Carly, keeping her voice quiet with warmth, wondering if she should have broken into Sam's trance.

Sam snapped back into the moment and smiled back at Carly, a little ashamed of herself for instantly wanting to dig into the fluffy tissue paper that peeked out from the bag in her hands. Carly sat next to Sam on the edge of the bed, gave her foot a loving squeeze, and handed her the gift. Sam delicately parted the tissue and pulled out the hardcover journal Carly had personalized just for her. She ran her fingers over the gold lettering, which lay over the rich royal blue cover.

"My dearest Sam, with faith and hope, and the power of your thoughts, your future belongs to you. Create, Dream and Enjoy."

"I hope you like it. I had a journal as a teenager and writing my feelings, and the goals I began to create for myself, allowed me to heal more thoroughly than anything else could."

"Heal from what?" asked Sam.

Up until now, Carly had kept her own past to herself, waiting for Sam acclimate to her new surroundings, and believe that her intentions were pure and worthy of Sam's trust. "I lived your life, Sam. My mother seemed to hate my very existence and I endured 16 years of my life in total isolation. Every day seemed more hopeless than the last, every beating became closer to the edge until one day, just before my rescue, I was sure my mother would not stop until I was dead."

Sam stared back at Carly in disbelief, looked into her teacher's watering eyes, and, for the first time, had hope that her own worthlessness could metamorphosis into something beautiful, something lovable and somebody who might be worthy of Daisy's admiration.

Sam didn't respond with words, but instead reached over and gripped her arms around Carly's shoulders, and squeezed until she was sure her appreciation resonated through the tight embrace. It was the first act of affection Sam had offered Carly since her salvation from her mother's prison.

"You're welcome, Sam," Carly said in return. "Try and get some sleep, tomorrow is a big day. For both of us."

Sam stayed up late, however, penning down the new story of her life until her hand ached from her feverish writing, which failed to keep up with her flooding thoughts. Her thoughts, although full of anticipation, were overridden with the terror of never seeing her Daisy again. She wouldn't allow herself to believe that nightmare was true, though, as she would never fully rest until her baby was safe in her embrace once more.

CHAPTER 32

Agents Cooper and Townsend walked slowly down the long corridor, passing a dozen empty cubby spaces as the click of their heels echoed out with authority after each deliberate step. They finally reached Arlene Beckensworth, looking straight at them through the protection of the sound and bulletproof glass, wearing the orange uniform of societies degenerates. They greeted her cordially with a nod of their heads.

Townsend sat down across from Arlene and picked up the phone to start their interview, as Cooper stood behind, legs firm and hip-width apart, his hands gripped together behind his arrow-straight back.

"Good afternoon, Mrs. Beckensworth."

Townsend waited for a reaction at the use of her legal name, but Arlene did not flinch. She instead stared back without so much as a blink of her eyes, her arrogance only intensifying through her silence and indignant posture.

"We have been looking for you for some time now, Arlene. Seems you can't run far enough from your troubles, as it turns out. You led us right to your front door."

Arlene held her phone to her ear without response, offering only her cold, hard stare in return.

"You need to tell me where to find Daisy, Arlene, and you need to tell me now."

Silence.

"Is she still alive?"

Silence.

"We have Jennifer's dress. We pulled your DNA, mixed with Jennifer's blood, from the dress just as we have matched your DNA with evidence found alongside the broken bones of your helpless daughter's remains. Your running is over."

Silence.

"We have a green light from the prosecutor's office to take our case to trial, as you already know from your formal arrest this morning for the murder of Jennifer

Beckensworth...once Michigan authorities are through with you here, that is."

Silence.

"So I will ask you again. Where is Daisy, Arlene?"

"I want my lawyer," was Arlene's only response, said playfully through the smirking of her lips as she fully enjoyed that only she possessed the knowledge everyone in town so desperately demanded.

"Of course. Disappointing, though. I was hopeful we could work together to get what we both want, as your cooperation with Daisy's return is your sole chance of getting a plea deal from the prosecutor in Kentucky, and, I can assure you, he is after nothing less than your blood. I will let him know you are uninterested," said Townsend firmly, before clicking his phone back into its receiver and standing up to leave.

Arlene jumped up and knocked against the glass to get the Agent's attention, and although the sound from her pounding knuckles was no match against the barrier in which she fought, Townsend saw her movement from the corner of his eye. He walked back to his seat and picked up his phone once more, just as a guard lowered Arlene back into her chair with the steady and downward pressure of his firm hand upon her bony shoulder.

"Yes?" Asked Townsend.

"What kind of deal?" Said Arlene.

"Not without your lawyer, my dear. I'll see you in Kentucky."

"Wait! Just wait," said Arlene impatiently. "I take it back. I waive my right to my lawyer right now. What kind of deal?"

Townsend kept his smile to himself and instead kept his demeanor steady as ever. "I can't tell you that. I've only been given the go-ahead to offer leniency if Daisy is recovered. The details of which will come after your cooperation."

Arlene sat still as she contemplated her next step.

"Is Daisy still alive?" Townsend asked with urgency, as his heart began to pulse quickly underneath the sudden weight of his suit coat.

"I don't know."

"How is it that you don't know, Mrs. Beckensworth?"

"I will only continue if you promise to keep me here. Jail is the only place I will be safe."

"I can assure you, ma'am, you aren't going anywhere but back to your cell," replied Townsend, hiding his growing contempt as Arlene's eyes filled effortlessly with tears.

"I met a man several months ago in my diner. Well, not *my* diner of course, but where I worked. We began dating pretty quickly and he seemed perfect at first. He treated me so kindly. Even after meeting my kids he was still interested, he seemed to really like them, even. Poor Daisy never had a father figure in her life, since her daddy took off as soon as I got pregnant, and I thought this guy could really be that for her, ya know?"

"What was this man's name?"

"Terrance, something. I don't know if he ever told me his last name, actually."

"You didn't know his last name, but you thought he could be a daddy to your little girl?" Townsend responded, instantly upset he spoke his thought out loud so carelessly. "I guess I can understand that, ma'am," he recovered, "I know how important it must be to find a decent man to share your life with."

"Impossible is more like it. There isn't no decent men left in this world, I swear to you. Decent and available, that is, no offense to you, of course."

"None taken. Please, continue."

"After a month or so, Terrance got real aggressive with me, insisting I do and say things that no woman should have to do, you know, in the bedroom. I tried to distance myself from him but I couldn't escape. He came to my home at all hours of the night, scaring my girls by poundin' every window of the house until I let him in. He showed up at my work and made terrible scenes, almost made me lose my job."

"Uh-huh," nudged Townsend, hoping she would soon get to the point.

"I went almost a week without hearing from him, and I thought he finally set me free. That is, until the day he showed up at my house, the day he took Daisy from me."

"Your boyfriend took Daisy? Why did you lie about her whereabouts, then? Why did you not seek the help from Detective Brody that very day, when he came to your house?"

"I couldn't." Terrance had finally told me the truth, told me that he was married. He said his wife couldn't get pregnant and they needed a daughter to call their own. He said he couldn't afford the steep adoption costs and so this was their only option. He promised that if I told anyone, that if he heard on the news that I had worked with the police, he would first kill Daisy, and then find Samantha and me. He promised he would rape and kill Samantha in front of my eyes, and then torture me until I died, too."

"Do you think he meant that?"

"I knew without a shred of doubt he meant it, and that he could do it, too. I knew first hand how sick his mind was, what disgusting things turned him on. Even if I did work with police, and they kept Samantha and I safe, I knew he would still kill Daisy. I couldn't risk it."

"Do you know where this man, Terrance, lived?"

"I have no idea. He always insisted on coming to my house."

"And what did he look like?"

Arlene detailed her fabricated boyfriends appearance, and kept it as close to Terry's actual features as she could recall, all the while pausing to blow her nose, or catch her breath, or to bow her head into her knees when the grief became too much to bare. All to enhance the believability of her incredible story.

"One more question, Mrs. Beckensworth. Where did you get the 20,000 dollars deposited into your bank account last week?"

Arlene became cold as stone once more from the icy tone of Townsend's doubtful voice.

"From my personal savings I hid under my mattress. I thought it about time I put my hard-earned money someplace more appropriate. Seems silly to me now, that I kept that kind of cash in such a vulnerable place, like I was just asking to be robbed. Is that all?"

"Yes, ma'am. We will be in touch."

"What about my deal?"

"We will be in touch," Townsend said once more, before ending the interview by aggressively hanging up his phone and storming off ahead of his partner.

After picking up a copy of the recorded interview Cooper finally turned his head toward Townsend as they walked out of the jailhouse. "Well?"

But Townsend was too wrapped up in his thoughts, in what worried him most, to respond. He had been at this game long enough to know that $20,000 was way too much money. Double, actually, the amount paid from broker to seller in every child trafficking case he had worked in the past.

Townsend felt the urgency to uncover the missing pieces of the case intensify after speaking with Arlene. His sense of a looming tragedy seemed to taunt Townsend's confidence, and fill his ears with a rhythmic tick—the sound of time running out.

CHAPTER 33

Sam stood in front of the long mirror Carly hung on the back of her bedroom door, and admired the image glowing back in return. The comfort Sam felt behind the safety of her room would crumble once she stepped through the doors of her Junior High, though. Best not to let confidence sneak through, Sam thought solemnly, as no matter what clothes she wore, her place as the school freak could never be undone.

Sam looked at the time and hurried herself down the stairs. She was running late already, and would not risk missing her daily call with Brody. He was ever patient with Sam's daily calls, and encouraged her to reach out anytime she needed to. And even though Sam knew Brody would keep his word to contact her the moment he knew anything at all, just hearing his voice, hearing him speak Daisy's name, was the only thing keeping Sam's days even remotely manageable.

"Morning, Babe. I made you scrambled eggs. Eat while they're hot," said Carly, as she handed Sam her phone before joining her for breakfast.

"Thank you," said Sam as she dialed Brody's cell.

"What did he have to say?"

"Nothing much. He couldn't talk right now but said he would be by after school," said Sam. She shrugged her shoulders as if to say no big deal, but she could hear the tension in Brody's voice, making the pit in her already anxious stomach feel unbearable. "I can't eat right now, I'm sorry. Is that okay?"

"Nervous jitters, huh? No problem, sweetie. I made you a nice big lunch to take to school, hopefully your nerves ease up by then."

"Yeah, hopefully."

"We never talked about how you want to handle the kids today, how you want to answer their questions. About you living here with me, that is. What do you think?"

"I haven't thought about it, really. I would rather not say anything at all."

"Well, I want you to be prepared for their curiosity, hon. You know how I understand your need for privacy, but the news has been reporting your mother's arrest all week. About her real identity, and how she is the prime suspect in Daisy's disappearance. And also, I'm afraid, about the abuse of you and Daisy, and the murder of her first daughter 12 years ago."

All the blood drained from Sam's face, turning it first a pale white and then a yellowish green, just before her dash into the bathroom to purge her mortification from the depths of her stomach. Carly knew instantly she should have prepared Sam for this sooner, that waiting until the morning of her return into a life interrupted, both the same and forever changed, was a mistake.

Carly walked into the bathroom and rubbed Sam's back as she hovered over the toilet. "It's okay, babe. I will call the school, and we'll take one more day off, spend one more day here by ourselves."

Sam stood up, flushed the toilet, and rinsed out her mouth at the bathroom sink. "It's fine. Tomorrow won't be any easier. I'd rather just go and get this over with."

Even though Brody had already confirmed what Sam found, solidified the horror she uncovered in the attic as the dress belonging to a sister she knew nothing about, she hadn't realized she would face the pretty people fully armed with the details of her nightmarish life. She didn't stand a chance.

"Are you sure?" Asked Carly.

"Yes. I'm sure."

Carly and Sam walked into the building together, earlier than any the rest of the students as Carly had much to prepare following her week hiatus, giving Sam time to catch up on her work in a quiet, judge-free classroom.

As the first few students shuffled through the door, Carly shot Sam a quick wink to reassure her, to confirm she would, indeed, make it through the upcoming hour. Before long, each desk was filled with its proper student, all of them eager to have Ms. Chandler back at school. However, none of them spoke to Sam, fueling the awkward energy in the room. Finally, Eileen broke through the thick tension as she entered the class and walked with defiance past her empty desk and gawking friends. She swooped down to Sam and gave her a huge hug full of genuine care. "Oh my god, Sam. You look amazing."

"Yeah, Sam! I almost didn't recognize you!" Josh Thompson exclaimed, facing her directly for the first time.

"I love your hair!" Said one girl.

"I love your shirt!" Said another.

And before Sam knew it, a murmur of affection swirled in and around her ears, bringing tears of constrained relief to her now glasses-free eyes. In fact, all but one of her classmates felt real empathy for Sam, but she did not even notice Amy sitting stiff as an arrow, rolling her eyes in disgust at each compliment thrown Sam's way.

Carly's heart swelled with love as she witnessed her class, these kids, giving Sam all that was still good in such a hardened world. She winked at Sam once more before gaining the attention of her students and getting class underway.

Sam continued the morning through a haze of disbelief. Sam reasoned to herself that this newfound acceptance, although still fragile and unsure, was due solely to her fashionable clothes and new hair-do. And while those things had much to do with it, her reception was more so in response to the new energy she offered through her love and self-acceptance, through the small truths she subconsciously began redefining herself with.

"Sam, wait up," said Eileen, as she jogged ahead, and linked her arm through Sam's as they walked into the lunchroom. "Sit with me?"

"Um, where?" Asked Sam.

"Anywhere. How about over there?" She said, as she pointed to an empty table across the cafeteria.

Sam followed without response, still unable to shake the fear of being led straight into ridicule yet again. She held her breath, clinging desperately to her intuition that Eileen was as genuine as she seemed, and only exhaled once the two were indeed seated alone and in peace.

"Is it true you are living with Ms. Chandler?" Eileen burst out, as she had been dying to get the details from Sam all day.

"Yes," answered Sam.

"Wow, you are so lucky! Is she as nice at home as she is in school? Is her house just beautiful? Does she have a boyfriend, I mean, how could she not?"

"Um, no. I mean, yes, her house is beautiful and she is really nice at home, nicer even, I think. But no, I don't think she has a boyfriend, I haven't asked, anyway, I would feel too weird bringing it up."

"Don't get me wrong, I love my parents," said Eileen, "but you are really lucky to have Ms. Chandler. Don't you think she is the prettiest woman you have ever seen? I used to wish for a mom just like her when I was really little."

"What do you mean?" Asked Sam. "I remember your mom, she always seemed perfect to me. I used to wish I had a mom like yours every time I left your house. Until she stopped letting you play with me, anyway."

"Oh, no, my mom really is great. I wouldn't say perfect," Eileen laughed, "but she is the best mom ever. I'm really lucky, too."

Sam shook her head and shrugged her shoulders with confusion.

"Will you keep a secret, Sam? Nobody knows...I wanted to tell somebody so bad, but I was afraid Amy would make everybody hate me if anybody knew the truth. But I don't care anymore. I don't have any real friends, anyway."

"You have tons of friends," Sam chuckled, not understanding what Eileen meant. Again.

"Sure seems that way. But not really. They all seem so fake. I mean, I hang out with those girls all the time, but usually I feel lonelier with them, than when I'm home alone. Crazy, right? Anyway, my parents aren't my real parents. I mean, they are my mom and dad, but they adopted me when I was five years old."

Before Sam could respond, Josh walked behind her and tapped the opposite shoulder from where he stood, laughing when she looked to see nobody there.

"Always the jokester, Josh," said Eileen with a roll of her eyes.

"This seat taken?" Asked Josh, before sitting down and possessing the spot next to Sam with the clunk of his lunch tray.

"Guess not," said Sam, feeling an overwhelming emotion mixed with both unease and a strange new delight.

By the end of the day, Sam's unexpected support did much to heal her aching heart, but she was too preoccupied with getting home to Detective Brody to think about the possibility of an actual friendship blooming through a shared past. Sam walked into Carly's classroom expecting her to be packed and ready to go, and tried to hide her frustration with Ms. Chandler's lack of urgency.

"I know you're eager to get home, babe, but I have a few things I absolutely must finish up before I can leave. If it makes you feel any better, Detective Brody won't be over until close to 5 o'clock, so we won't keep him waiting, k?"

"Okay, of course, no problem."

"Want to keep me company while you wait?"

"Do you mind if I sit outside on the bench in front of the school? I could use some fresh air."

"Sounds great. I won't be too long, I promise," Carly assured Sam, as she headed towards the door.

Sam sat cross-legged on the metal bench, letting the late afternoon sun beat down a comforting warmth around her shoulders, which helped keep the battle of her thoughts in a positive place. If Brody had good news, he would have shared it right away, she thought. But so too would he tell her if something were wrong, he wouldn't make her wait through a day at school first, she reasoned.

Lost deep in her worry, Sam didn't notice the black sedan that pulled up around the horseshoe drive that looped in front of the school doors.

"Sam," called out a man's voice through the unrolled passenger side window.

Sam looked up, startled, and recognized Detective Brody's partner summoning her toward his car.

"Yeah?" Sam replied, as the hair on her arms and neck stood at full attention, screaming at her to run back into the school.

"You must come to the station with me right away. It's Daisy. Brody sent me to get you."

"What happened?" Yelled Sam, "What is it!"

"You need to hurry. Now."

"Okay, let me run and tell Ms. Chandler, I'll be right back."

"We don't have time for that, Daisy needs you NOW. Brody is on the phone with Ms. Chandler as we speak, she'll meet us there."

And without a shred of hesitation Sam ran into Jackson's car. The second her door was shut Jackson sped frantically from the school parking lot, and didn't slow down until they were miles away, traveling along a freeway headed in the opposite direction from their town.

"Drink this," demanded Jackson.

"No thank you, I'm not thirsty," said Sam, even though she had to force down each swallow through the sandpaper coating of her dry throat.

"I said drink it."

And when Sam did not respond, did not budge, Jackson un holstered his gun and held it toward her head, all without ever taking his eyes off the road.

"Drink."

And Sam obeyed, fully realizing the real danger she was in.

CHAPTER 34

Brody slipped his phone into the pocket that hid beneath his suit jacket as he hurried down the hall to the conference room. He felt guilty for rushing Sam through their conversation, as if he broke his promise to always talk her through her worries, but the Federal Agents were waiting and he needed to deal with the information he had received without delay.

"Morning, Detective," greeted Townsend.

"Good Morning. Sorry I'm a bit late, I had to take a call."

"No problem, I'm still getting set up anyhow. Is everything okay? Where is Detective Jackson?"

"He didn't tell you?" Asked Brody.

"Tell me what, exactly?"

"Jackson has taken an extended leave of absence, I'm afraid. Minimum of six months. You and Agent Cooper will be working with just me from here on out."

"Eh," replied Townsend, "No real loss if you ask me. There was something about him, man thought he was too smart for his own good."

"I know what you mean. I need to run something by you before we get started. The call I had to take was from Jackson's old department in Nevada—"

"Oh?" Interrupted Townsend.

Agent Cooper paused from setting up the tape recorder and looked up. "What did they want?"

"Well, I left a message with the department first, actually, and have been waiting for the Chief to return my call. I did some digging into Jackson's work history and found he had served as a Detective with the Las Vegas Special Victims Unit almost ten years ago. I thought it odd he had never mentioned it because he bragged—constantly—about all the departments he had worked for, all over the country, but deliberately left this one out. So I called."

"And?" Said Townsend.

"And he was terminated. That's all I know. The chief wouldn't give me further details, though I could tell he wanted to. Seems odd he didn't mention his experience working the SVU, as it relates so closely to this case."

"Interesting," said Cooper, his face tight with disdain.

"Yeah. Anyway, what do we have?"

"Right. I interviewed Arlene Beckensworth yesterday afternoon. I want you to review the recording with us. Maybe you'll pick up on something I missed."

"Can't wait," said Brody, as he sat anxiously down at the long, ominously empty conference table.

The three men sat closely together around the tape recorder and listened as the sound of Arlene's voice chilled the air around them.

Townsend paused the recording just as Arlene began her account of Daisy's kidnapping. "What struck me right away was before Arlene would talk, she insisted on reassurance of her safety. But never did she mention her fear for her children, or question how we would keep them safe based on this man's threats. I would think, if her story is indeed the truth, she would also request the safety of Samantha, request that we keep the details quiet in order to protect Daisy. But she doesn't, and I believe she overlooked their safety for two reasons. One, she really doesn't care about her children, as we already know, and two, her story is bull shit."

Brody was listening, but could not tear his eyes away from the single word he wrote in his notes.

"Wouldn't you agree, Brody?"

"Please, continue the tape," was his response.

Cooper looked over at Townsend with confusion as he hit play, wishing he were piecing together what Brody already seemed on to.

"And what did he look like?"

"He was tall and skinny, weak looking. That was one of the reasons I was so surprised at how easily he could overtake me when I wouldn't do as he said in the bedroom. Looking back, he wasn't even good looking. I don't know what drew me to him in the first place."

"Can you describe his facial features?"

Of course, I could never forget his face. His head was long and narrow, and his chin seemed to end in a point, like an exclamation mark following down from his wide forehead. His nose was large and slightly crooked; the way it jutted out from his face reminded me of a parrot's beak. I imagined breaking it with my fist many times."

"What color was his hair?"

"Jet black. He always kept it greased up and slicked back. I learned early to never touch his hair or else he would freak out."

"Stop the tape."

Cooper stopped the recording, and both agents looked at Brody's pale face as he held up his note pad.

TERRANCE.

"Terrance. Terry Jackson. She is describing Detective Jackson."

Brody jumped from his chair and charged towards his Lieutenant's office, as Townsend and Cooper followed.

"What is it, Brody?" Asked the Lieutenant, as the three men barreled through his door before he could respond to Brody's urgent knock.

"We have our man. I need Jacksons personnel file immediately."

The Lieutenant didn't hesitate, he trusted and knew Brody enough not to question his request. He phoned down to human resources to pull the file, and Townsend and Cooper filled him in as Brody hurried to retrieve the information.

When Brody returned, the agents quickly spoke their next plan of action, as two uniformed officers waited for their orders outside of the office. Brody wrote down the address listed in Jackson's file, and the three men fled the station to bring Jackson in for questioning while the Lieutenant called in an emergency search warrant request to the judge.

The men arrived to the address, just ten miles away, in less than 10 minutes, as Brody sped down the highway as quickly as safety would allow.

"No fucking way," Brody blurted out in frustration, ending the silence that had consumed the car throughout the entire drive. They matched the address to a house with a "For Rent" sign mocking them in the front yard.

They exited the car in unison and Cooper wrote down the phone number listed on the sign as Townsend and Brody looked into the house through the curtain-less front window.

"Empty," Townsend called to Cooper.

Brody tested the front door but it was locked, as was the garage and back door. Brody peeked in through the back door window, but the kitchen, too, was gutted and empty. He walked back around the house to peer through every window, all confirming no signs of life.

"God *dammit*," Brody mumbled, as he rejoined Agent Townsend in the front yard. He phoned the Lieutenant to halt the police officers in-route, and requested them instead investigate tirelessly until Jackson's last known address was found. Just as he hung up, Cooper joined the two men standing beside the "For Rent" sign, with information of his own.

"I reached the owner of the house. No surprise that it isn't Jackson. But the landlord did remember him. Jackson and his wife rented the place awhile ago, five years he estimated, but abruptly broke their lease and moved out."

"Did the landlord happen to obtain a forwarding address for them?" Asked Brody.

"Nope, I asked. He said that Jackson had paid through the rest of the lease agreement with cash, in full, so he said there was no need."

"Of course he did," replied Townsend. "So now what," he thought out loud, as the men walked toward the car to return to the station.

By the time the team returned, the briefing room was abuzz with officers, their Lieutenant, and the Chief of Police. White flip charts with the case notes were displayed on either side of the bulletin board, which covered the front wall of the room. Pinned to it were pictures of Jennifer, Arlene, and Chad Beckensworth, Samantha and Daisy Beckett, a printed question mark indicating Daisy's father as unknown, and Detective Jackson glaring in his uniform blues.

Brody, along with the Agents, joined the Lieutenant and Chief whom already stood at their place of authority in front of a dozen eager officers, sitting two to a desk, with their notepads ready.

"We will keep this brief and to the point," said the Chief as he called the meeting to order. "We have sufficient reason to believe that Detective Terrance Jackson is behind, or somehow involved, in the disappearance and possible kidnapping of Daisy Beckett.

"His address on file is a dead end," added Brody. "He left that residence as long as five years ago, we've gathered. Who is assigned to track down a current address?" Brody nodded his head toward the raised hands in back. "Good, you two are dismissed. Get on it."

"Now," said Brody, "Who has been investigating the pre-paid phone sales?"

"We have," said a team sitting in the front desk.

"And?"

"There wasn't as many sales to filter through as we had anticipated, which made things a whole lot easier. One transaction, or should I say a series of transactions, stood out.

Two weeks before Arlene Beckensworth made the call to the phone number in question; there was a sale of a Celebrate Wireless prepaid service from the Smithsville County Shop-Mart, the only one that day, actually. The phone was purchased first with a credit card, then returned, and resold with cash—same serial number."

"And," said Brody, impatiently.

"We have subpoenaed the credit card details, along with the store's video surveillance from that day. We are just waiting for the information to come through from their corporate office, should be any day."

"We don't have "any day." Both of you drive there now, show the manager a copy of the subpoena, and don't leave until you have the information in your hands. And call me as soon as you do."

"Yes, sir," they said in unison, before rising from their desk and heading out the door.

Brody ignored the vibration of his phone, yelling at him from beneath his jacket as he continued.

A young officer, fresh faced and squeaky clean in his rookie year, raised his hand.

"Yes?"

"I have been working on finding the identity and whereabouts of Daisy Beckett's father. So far I have come up empty. Her birth certificate lists the father as unknown, and the hospital records show that Arlene, AKA Beth, gave birth without the father present. I'm not sure where to look from here," he finished, his face suddenly flushed with embarrassment.

"Go dig through the case file, there are hundreds of letters written by Arlene that we recovered from her home. You might find something there."

The rookie didn't move, just nodded his head in understanding.

"Waiting for something?" Said Brody.

"Oh, right," said the young man, hitting his long legs beneath the desk as he jolted up, flushing deeper still, as his peers chuckled around the room.

"That's enough," said Brody, ignoring the persistent vibration upon his chest once more. "Who else has something to offer?"

The department's most seasoned officer raised his hand. I received, just today, a copy of the entire cold case file, originally opened 12 years ago, regarding the disappearance of Chad Beckensworth's. The sheriff's department in Kentucky has been extremely cooperative, thanks to Agent Townsend," he said, while thanking Townsend with a nod of his head.

"No trouble at all," Townsend returned.

"Start combing through the file immediately. Seems everyone close to Arlene goes missing, and that is certainly no coincidence. A fresh set of eyes might be just what's needed to give that department, and the Beckensworth family, some closure."

Brody took a short pause to look at his caller ID, as his phone buzzed at him for a third time, demanding it not be ignored. He looked down at the name, Carly Chandler, and even amidst the urgency of this new lead, his heart jumped itself straight into his throat and throbbed with immediate longing. Unable to risk further distraction, he sent her call to voicemail and called his attention back to the waiting officers.

"The rest of you, all of you, research everything you can find on child trafficking, not just here but nationwide. Do not stop until you have read every case available, until you can certify yourself as an expert, and until you have not only an acute and intimate knowledge of how these rings work, but also on how to track them down. Dismissed."

As the remaining officers shuffled out the door to get working on their assignment, the

Lieutenant's secretary weaved her way through the crowd and into the room.

"Detective Brody, I have a Carly Chandler on the line. She says it is imperative she speak with you right away."

Brody knew instantly that he should have taken her call. "Put her through to my desk," he said as he jogged past her, already on his way out the door.

"Hello?"

"Brody! It's Sam! She's gone!"

"Where are you?"

"At the school. I have the whole faculty looking. She is not here! Oh my god, Brody. She's gone!"

"Stay put. I'm on my way."

CHAPTER 35

In the week since Angel's breakdown on the floor of Terry's office, she had avoided Daisy as much as possible. She tried to distance herself from the heartbreak, from the horror, and from the demonic claws thirsting for the sweet innocence of a child.

Now she went down into the cellar only to offer enough food and hydration to keep Daisy alive. Terry beat her after the blanket episode, only to thank her afterward for keeping their investment profitable. He apologized for losing his temper, and placed a gentle kiss on her head as a reward for her quick action, for thinking on her feet. He even let Daisy keep the blanket to keep warm, which, to Angel, was worth the fresh bruises that covered over remnants of old, long since received, but never quite healed.

Angel sat at the edge of her bed for several minutes, still loosely wrapped in her sleeping pill haze, before finding the strength to move her aching body to feed Daisy. Knowing she must be starving, as Terry stopped allowing her food past 10am, she willed herself up to prepare breakfast.

"Hello?" Daisy whispered, too weak to sit up.

Angel set her food down beside her, like a dog, without speaking a word.

"Ms. Angel?" Daisy called out.

Angel, with her back turned to Daisy, closed her eyes and bowed her head in sadness. She took a deep breath and continued with her task in order to break free from the cellar, and from her breaking heart. Holding her hand in the bottom of a plastic bag, Angel bent down in the tight space behind the stairs and picked up Daisy's waste, and quickly knotted the handles together as she wrenched out a gag from her weak stomach.

Daisy began to cry from embarrassment. "Sorry, Ma'am," she wept out.

Angel fought back her own tears as she walked up the stairs, taking each step desperately slow as the pain in her shins burned down to the core of her bones, her fresh bruises from Terry's steel-toe boots throbbing in agony with each steep climb upward.

Daisy pushed herself up into a sitting position, finding her strength through the smell of her food, peanut butter and jelly melted between a hot english muffin. "Ms. Angel? Please wait..."

Angel paused midway up the stairs, but didn't turn to face the soft voice below, a voice cracking through each word as it fought against the sadness of a little girls broken heart.

"You don't like me anymore, just like momma. And I know why," Daisy said softly through her tears, "I tried hard to be good."

Angel's tears released down her cheeks as she held herself steady with the palm of her hand against the dusty wall. "This isn't your fault, Daisy. None of it."

"Sammy told me how to be a good girl...but I am dirty rotten like mama says."

Angel fought against her better judgment and slowly walked to Daisy's side, tugged on the edge of the blanket to smooth out a space, and sat down to cradle her battered arm around Daisy's fragile shoulders. As Daisy nuzzled her head against Angel's beating heart, the two cried together, as both needed comfort, needed absolute love, just as desperately as the other.

"You are a good girl, Daisy. The best little girl I have ever met, I promise you that. Don't believe your mama, sweety. There's nothin' rotten about you, nothin' at all."

"Then why did you stop talkin' to me? Is it cause Uncle Terry comes down here when it's dark?"

Angel felt her last thread of hope snap furiously apart from the mounting strain of shame's heavy weight, the despair on Daisy's face too much for her to bare. Since the day she rescued Daisy from the cellar's chill, the day she let Daisy's affection sneak in and settle possessively in her chest, Angel made sure she got to Terry first every night. She seduced him through his power-driven fantasies, and kept him going as long as her body would allow, spilling his needs fully before his urges tugged him down into the darkness of his lust. Before it lured him down the cellar steps and into Daisy's innocence, stealing away the purity of her heart forever.

"You are a good girl, you will always be a good girl, no matter what happens, okay? I didn't mean to hurt your feelings, I just have to do what Terry says. Does that make sense?"

Daisy nodded her head. "I won't never tell Uncle Terry you're nice, I promise. I can keep a secret really good."

Angel unwrapped her arm from around Daisy and offered her breakfast once more. "It's getting cold, you should eat."

Daisy picked up her sandwich with both her chubby little hands and took a huge bite, smiling up at Angel as she struggled to chew the mouthful, too big for her little mouth.

"I'm sorry Uncle Terry came down to you. That isn't your fault, either. I tried as best I could to keep him away. Did he hurt you?"

Daisy's cheeks turned a rosy pink underneath the layers of dirt, as she forced the peanut butter down her throat with a big gulp of water. "No ma'am. He didn't hurt me. Sam warned me before about mama's boyfriends. And I am brave just like her."

"Braver even, I bet." Angel picked up Daisy's doll and placed it in her lap. "I have to go now, Terry will be home soon. Remember our secret, Daisy. He can't ever know we talk to each other. Not ever."

Daisy smiled while hugging her doll and happily nodded her head up and down, eager at the chance to please Ms. Angel.

Angel left yet another piece of her heart with Daisy as she walked up the steps, just as painful as during her first attempt, wiping out the little energy she had left. Once locking the cellar door, she fell limp into the closest kitchen chair, her face falling straight into the palms of her hands as she contemplated her only option besides death. How far could she get with Daisy before Terry came looking, she thought. She slowly raised her head and dragged her hands down the length of her face before letting them fall onto the table, and on top of a stack of papers she had not noticed until now.

"What the hell?"

———— ♦ ————

Jackson tilted Samantha's head onto a pillow against the passenger side window, making it seem as if she were merely resting and not passed out from his potent sleep concoction, perfected over years of trial and error. He drove them down a remote road lined on each side with dense woods and over-brush, and stopped at his favorite hiding spot. He almost drove past the small carpool parking lot, it's entrance concealed by tall weeds from years of neglect. It sat waiting for him—long forgotten by others—tucked out of sight behind century old pine trees, standing tall with wisdom, encircling the entire gravel enclosure.

Sam's head fell forward with only her seatbelt keeping her body in place, as the car bounced up and over the overgrowth and down into the gravel pit below. Small pebbles crunched and popped under the car's weight as Terry rolled into his spot, completely concealed from the road, and slowly shifted the car into park.

"Here we are sweet thing. We have quite a few hours to kill before dark. I can't go carrying you into my home in broad daylight, now can I? No, of course not."

Terry turned Sam's unconscious face toward his own, stroking her cheek with his thin thumb. "You're just dying for me, aren't you? Your mother told me what a slut you are, always luring her boyfriends wandering eyes toward your own body. Flaunting your youth in her face. Not that your mother is any prize worth winning, she's as used up as I've seen."

Terry filled the car with sadistic laughter before parting Samantha's lips with his own, while his hand traveled down her blouse and under her bra, and squeezed her flesh until his mark was solidified upon her body from the fingertip shaped bruises he left behind.

"We are going to have fun, you and I. Just you wait," said Terry while unzipping his slacks, no longer able to resist his throbbing need as he imagined Sam's voice, his new possession, screaming out for mercy through unspeakable pain.

Still feeling unsatisfied after releasing just enough pressure to take the edge off his demanding desires, Terry got out of the car and paced back and forth, imagining the gravel which crunched beneath his feet were the fragmented remains of Brody pummeled face, ripped apart by Terry's own hands.

He dug his phone from his front pocket and dialed home.

"Pack your bags. We leave tomorrow."

———— ◆ ————

Angel hug up the phone and continued to pace the house, her terror pulsating through her veins in rhythm with her rapid pulse. Terry's call confirmed that she, too, would be taken overseas. She wandered into the kitchen, her racing mind reaching madness, as she looked out the window and into the soft orange glow of the setting sun. She realized at once there was no time left to leave Terry's prison; no time for her to escape with

Daisy far enough from Terry's deeply connected reach.

She sat defeated at the kitchen table, picking up once more her discovery from earlier that day. Four passports, three with pictures she recognized as herself, Terry, and Daisy, the fourth of a little girl she had never seen before. All four documents sharing the same fictitious last name. "The Weston's," Angel said out loud, "The All American Family."

She breathed in and out in a steady rhythm, telling herself Terry would not force her into prostitution again. And to be honest, that was the least of her worries. Maybe it was good she was going along, maybe she could offer Daisy the comfort of familiarity during her initiation, during the filth that her tender heart will have to endure, breaking her perfect spirit for the rest of her life.

Angel didn't move from the kitchen table for hours, trapped inside a comatose state consumed with swirling thoughts, her mind flipping back and forth between fantasy and reality, until the dark of night filled the room. The slam of Terry's car door from the driveway brought her close to the surface of real-life. The slam of the second door, however, fully snapped

Angel out of her dream-filled confusion as she dashed up and flipped on the light switch.

Terry twisted the handle of the kitchen doorknob with one hand, as he balanced Samantha's body with the other. He kicked open the door with the bottom of his foot, sending it flying open with anger before slamming into the wall. He walked in carrying his cumbersome new addition and glared at Angel, evil satisfaction glinting from his eyes.

"Surprise, darling."

"Surprise, indeed," Angel responded, still not entirely sure she was not still dreaming.

"Meet Samantha. She should be coming to any minute now," Terry said, waving Sam's limp hand at Angel with his own.

"Samantha? As in Daisy's sister?"

"Of course. You didn't think I was going to just watch my money be pissed away, did you? I already paid that whore up front for both kids, she already belonged to me. Poor thing was living the high life in some rich woman's house, too. She's going to wake up devastated," Terry laughed, "will serve her right for thinking she belonged in a place like that."

"Right," agreed Angel. "She is sure in for a surprise."

Terry laughed again, fully pleased with himself, and gestured toward Angel as if to say, 'get off your fat ass and open the cellar door', to which she immediately obeyed. "Go get my briefcase from my car, and make me a drink before I come back up."

As Terry pulled the string hanging from the single dusty bulb to light his downward path, Angel shut the door and leaned her back against it to slow her panicked heart.

She knew what she had to do.

CHAPTER 36

Brody screeched up to the school and slammed his brakes, sending the squealing wail of his arrival in front of the main double doors. Carly was outside waiting for him, smoking a cigarette she had bummed from the custodian, and shaking from her absolute knowledge that Sam had been taken, and that it was she who failed to keep her safe.

As Brody ran to Carly she dropped the cigarette and smashed it under her foot, embarrassed at being caught in her old habit. She hadn't smoked in years, but was unable to resist her nerves screaming out for relief.

"Brody, I am so sorry. I let this happen," Carly sobbed, sending Brody closer still as he wrapped his sturdy arms around her trembling back until her body stopped jerking underneath the comfort of his authoritative embrace.

"This isn't your fault, Carly. Sit down," he said as he led her to the bench where Sam had sat just an hour before. "Where did you see Sam last?"

Carly calmly told Brody of her last conversation with Sam, and apologized over and over again for not making Sam stay put beneath the safety of her careful watch.

"You couldn't have known, Carly. I didn't even realize Sam's safety was in jeopardy until the very second your call came through to the station. We know who took her, now we just have to find him."

Carly's head snapped up as she looked into the steady depth of Brody's eyes, warming further as he looked into the beauty of her own tear-filled blues. "Who!" Carly demanded.

"Detective Jackson," he said, as his entire body went stiff from speaking his partner's name. "If anyone is to blame, it's me. I should have looked into his past long before now. I knew he wasn't who he claimed, and yet I let that monster continue to prey for his victims in my own community, right under my nose."

"Oh my God. How do you know? And what are we doing sitting here, then? Let's go get him!"

"Trust me, we have every last resource looking for him. Based on what we now know, wherever he is living is surely under an alias name. But we will find him, Carly. I promise we will find him."

Carly's body began to violently vibrate once more, sending Brody's hands over her own, until his phone rang and broke their embrace with the promise of information.

"Brody," he answered.

"Agent Townsend, here. We have something."

Brody looked over at Carly, his eyes unable to conceal the flash of hope that bolted through his otherwise stoic expression, before he rose to walk toward his car.

"What is it?"

"We have confirmed that Jackson is not actually married. There is no marriage certificate on file, anywhere in the country."

"Ok," Brody replied, unsure of how helpful that information was.

"We have assumed that wherever he is living is under the name of his pseudo wife, as her name would not trace back to him, should someone come looking."

"Agreed..." Said Brody, still waiting for more.

"Also, I sent Agent Cooper to the Smithville Shop-Mart with your officers, to expedite through the bureaucracy of their privacy policies. And we have a name from the credit card sale. Angelica Palmer. Video surveillance showed the woman making the purchase in question wearing what appears to be a black wig, and round black sunglasses large enough to cover the better portion of her face. The tape also shows it was raining that day...anyway, does that name ring any bells?"

"I don't think so...wait. Angelica..." Brody was silent for a moment; something about the name seemed to fit. "Angel," he finally said out loud. "Jackson mentioned the name Angel not too long ago. Said it was some woman obsessed with him who couldn't take a hint, someone he was trying to get rid of.

"Get rid of," said Townsend.

"Exactly."

Brody had hoped the information would lead them to a more hopeful place. And as tangible as the new lead was, it also deepened the urgency of time, intensified the dangerous hands these two little girls were in.

"We have all hands on deck here, Brody. Every officer is checking on records for Angelica and any alias that fits closely to it. I will give them the name Angel to hone in on as well. How are things at the school?"

"Fine. Nothing here to go on so far."

"I'll keep in touch," said Townsend.

Brody hung up the phone as he returned to Carly. She held a small heart shaped pendant, which hung from a long silver chain and slowly swung back and forth in her hand.

"I found this hanging from the bench," Carly said, as she pointed to the rod-iron armrest. "Sam had it clipped to the zipper of her backpack. I bought it for her as a symbol of Daisy's heart, to give her something to hold, something to cling to, a reminder to stay hopeful."

Brody took the pendant from her hand and examined the bent link. "Must have ripped off when she left with Jackson," he said.

"Or when she was taken by him," Carly refuted.

"I don't think so. Jackson wouldn't risk making a scene. More likely she recognized him and went freely."

Brody searched the rest of the school for anything more that could help, but came up empty. He met Carly back in her classroom and helped gather her things before insisting he drive her home, not trusting her state of mind to get behind the wheel.

Then, once inside her home, Brody sat Carly down on her couch, its generous burgundy cushions hugging her in return, and covered her trembling body with the afghan that decorated the sitting chair beneath the room's grand window. "I'll be right back, I need to make a call."

"I will be fine, Brody. I am fine. You should go, I'm sure they need you at the station."

Brody resisted his urge to kiss Carly until her worries dissolved into passion from his lips, but knew she would never reciprocate his selfish desires in the midst of crisis, which peaked higher with anxiety through each passing moment. He, too, was fighting the desperation of time running out, but was trained to hide his emotions until the case was solved.

"Don't worry," Brody finally responded. I assure you, the station is in able hands. I will be back in a few minutes."

Carly was relieved, selfishly so, but felt connected to Samantha's safety in the presence of Brody's confident ability. She felt herself losing control of her yearning emotions as well, and the last layer of her heart that remained hardened and untrusting, and unable to break free from the walls built during the pain of her youth, began to fall away. Brick by brick.

Brody returned to the sitting room to find Carly lost in thought, her shoulders just slightly relaxed, despite her crisscrossed legs trembling and sweating beneath the warmth of the heavy blanket on top. "Anything new?" She asked.

"Not yet. No worries though, these things take time. We are a lot further along than we were this morning, however."

"That sounds encouraging," she said, offering nothing more but silence, each hearing only the begging of their own hearts beating in their ears to the point of total distraction.

"Where is your friend, what's his name? Todd?"

"Yes, Todd. He's away on vacation, I forget where. He isn't home very often at all, really."

"Are you two..."

"Together?" Carly finished.

"I'm sorry, it's none of my business."

"Todd is away with his new boyfriend," Carly smiled, "or boy-toy is probably more accurate. He is not much for commitment, that one."

"Oh, I see," Brody said, his relief plain for her to see. He moved closer to Carly as she told him the story of her life and Todd's role as her saving grace, opening up his mind's eye to Carly's heart and where her devotion for Samantha's well-being came from. He suddenly understood the beautiful miracle of Carly's resilient spirit, weaved together with honor, love and absolute gratitude.

"How about you, Brody...what's your story? You know all there is to know about me, and I don't even know your first name," Carly laughed, easing the tension she had created in the room.

"Theodore," Brody returned. "Theodore Edwin Brody. My friends called me Teddy as a kid."

"Teddy," Carly smiled. "Perfectly fitting."

Unable to stop him self this time, he held Carly's face between his strong hands, and watched her playful smile fade into sudden need as her eyes softened with desire. He leaned toward her until his lips met hers and parted them open with the soft demand of his tongue, until the ferocity of their need took control, plunging their mouths deeper into the other, each unable to satisfy their demand for more.

Brody pushed Carly's back into the armrest of the couch, his passion commanding her body as he yanked her blouse up from the waist of her skirt, fueled beyond reason to feel the silk of her flesh beneath his calloused hands. Carly arched her back from the pleasure of his touch as a lustful groan escaped her disobedient lips, pushing Brody's control to the very limits of his reach. He slowed his kiss, pulling with lust on her bottom lip before trailing his attention to the crook of her neck as he breathed in her scent, rich and warm like vanilla almond laced with cinnamon spice. Just as his hand found her ample breast, heaving impatiently from the entrapment of her bra, Brody's phone rang. It's shrill ring echoed through the open space, scolding him for what he had just done.

He leapt from the couch, grabbed his phone, and walked away to clear his head before he dared answer the call. "Brody, here. Yes. I'm on my way." He walked back to Carly as she tried to re pin the pieces of hair, which had escaped and fell beautifully around her face, still flushed with lust and confusion. "You are beautiful," he said, before he turned his heel and walked out the front door.

CHAPTER 37

Angel's plan rested in the hands of Terry and how long he would remain in the cellar. If he came back up too quickly and caught her in the act, she would be dead, no doubt about it. She had worn through every last one of Terry's threats, and this would push her beating beyond his usual self-control. She knew—with absolute certainty— that this time he would not stop until he punched into her body long after she had taken her last breath. But knowing Terry's mind, knowing just how completely his darkness had taken over, she knew what she had to do. Knew it the second he walked through the door carrying another helpless victim, unable to allow Daisy to witness her beloved sister become brutally victimized by the monster Angel had once loved.

Angel ran to Terry's car, as he instructed, and retrieved his briefcase from the back seat. As quickly as she could, she dashed back into the kitchen, set the briefcase on the table, and opened the tall cabinet above the stainless steel stove. As she reached for Terry's favorite Brandy snifter she began to tremble, and almost shattered it against the ceramic floor as her hands shook in terror. Once reclaiming the glass in her hands just in time, she set it next to the briefcase and filled it with Brandy, Terry's special bottle he had saved for when the time was just right. She clicked open the briefcase, took out his sleeping potion, and quickly poured its large remains into the snifter, not knowing how much would be sufficient enough to fully knock him out.

———— ◆ ————

Daisy kept her eyes shut tight as the sudden light poured down the steps and into her dungeon, knowing it was only Terry that came down to her during the night.

"Open your eyes little girl. I have a surprise for you."

Daisy squeezed her eyes even tighter, hoping Terry would think she was asleep and leave her alone.

"I said open your eyes," Terry yelled, kicking her in the stomach with the toe of his shoe. "Don't play games with me."

Daisy slowly obeyed, trying to focus on Terry as her eyes stung in response to the artificial light so seldom allowed. She squinted until the girl in his arms came into focus, although still unable to recognize the slumped shape as that of her Sam.

"Well," said Terry, unhappy with Daisy's underwhelmed reaction. "A bit of gratitude is in order, I'd say."

"Thank you, Uncle Terry," Daisy immediately responded, knowing from the tone in his voice she must say so, although confused as to why.

"Thank you? Is that all? After the danger I faced to bring her here? Worthless and ungrateful, indeed," Terry scolded, before bending down to spit in her face, spraying his contempt across her cheeks as she looked up in a plea for mercy.

"Thank you so much, I mean," Daisy quickly responded. "Thank you a lot. I really mean it, I promise."

Samantha, still limp from the weight of her numbed limbs, felt her heart beating through her chest and into Terry's as he carried her toward her waiting confinement, laughing wickedly all the while. She heard her baby's voice which confirmed what she already knew through the magnetic pull of their souls, connected back together as instantly as the cellar door flung open. Sam dared not move, however, even if she could. She did not dare open her eyes, and concentrated intently through her clouded thoughts to keep breathing as light and shallow as her body would allow.

Terry dropped Samantha's dead weight to the concrete floor below, her casted arm landing straight upon the rusted shackle, sending pain searing through her healing bones. Through the grace of God, and the lasting remains of her numbed senses, she remained lifeless, without so much as a flutter of her moist eyes. She fought back against the downpour of her waiting tears as Terry drug her body into position, leaving a trail of disruption behind as the grime beneath her body now rested atop her new clothes. He tightly secured the shackles just above Sam's feet until the cold iron pressed unforgivingly into her bony ankles, and the rusted metal dug into her flesh until drops of her bright-red blood rolled down to the dirt below.

Satisfied that Sam was sufficiently trapped, he turned his attention back to Daisy as he brushed the dust from his expensive slacks. "Don't you move a muscle until I get back, you hear? Do not touch her, do not go near her. Do not even speak a word to her, you understand?"

"Yes, sir," Daisy confirmed, still unable to recognize her Sammy under the new clothes, and her short hair which lay forward, obscuring her face from view. But for reasons Daisy didn't understand, she wanted nothing more than to be in the embrace of the girl locked in the chains. Wanted to hug and kiss her, and never let her go.

"I'll be back shortly. Remember what I told you to practice? Well, my little girl, you better have practiced," he said, grinning half in anticipation, half in self-satisfaction as he climbed his way to the kitchen to deal with Angel for one last night.

Terry slowly slid the lock back into place before fluidly turning toward Angel, with his weight rocked back on the heel of his right shoe. "Good Girl," he said to Angel as she sat patiently waiting, warming his brandy beneath the palms of her obedient hands. Terry sat as Angel offered his drink, and remained silent until the first sip burned down his throat and warmed the blood that flowed through his now lucid body.

"I see you found the passports. Surprised?"

"Quite," Angel responded, still imagining Terry charging with his hands outstretched toward her fragile neck.

"Thought it'd be too suspicious, me traveling alone with two young girls in light of a new missing child and all. The media is likely salivating as we speak, pretending to give a shit about a happy ending, all the while hoping for what really brings in their ratings. And I'm the bad guy," Terry laughed, before taking another sip. He swallowed hard and looked down into the deep burgundy as he swirled the drink beneath his nose.

"Of course. It's brilliant us traveling as a family," Angel replied, trying to distract Terry's current train of thought. "Will be a nice getaway for us, too."

"Yeah," laughed Terry. "A getaway, indeed."

Through the wicked spark in Terry's eyes as he laughed, Angel knew her fate was as she imagined, that her gut reaction was indeed correct. That his plans for her travelling along meant more than just the softness a mother's presence offered to a curious public looking in. And as Terry finished the remains of his Brandy in one last greedy gulp, a calm defiance rested upon Angel's steady shoulders, fueling her courage to stand tall in the storm of Terry's control. She calmly stood to refill Terry's empty glass, and steadily poured as his head bobbed sleepily up and down.

"What the hell," he said, shaking his head back and forth in an attempt to stop the fatigue which quickly gripped his mind in the claws of its deathly grasp. He looked down into his fresh drink, his mind fogging completely under the mist of his confusion as he took another sip. Only this time undiluted, it's true flavor burst through his mouth as it slid over his tongue, snapping Terry back into consciousness through the realization of what just happened.

"What the hell did you do!" Terry yelled, as he rose up from his chair, dropping the snifter from his weak hand as he wobbled to and fro on unsteady feet, his beloved crystal crashing to the floor. The warm liquid pooled around his feet and slowly rolled toward the cellar door, staining the white grout the color of old blood. Terry attempted to charge forward but his legs remained stuck, unwilling to obey his raging command. "You're DEAD!" He screamed, while dropping to his knees before he fully crashed onto the hard ceramic floor, his head landing firmly into the shards of broken glass. Blood oozed from his broken nose and gashed forehead towards the cellar door, bright red over a burnt brown path.

Angel grabbed the cast iron frying pan from the kitchen sink and struck Terry's head as hard as she could, struggling just slightly underneath its cumbersome weight. Then, as Angel ran toward the girls, the pan flew out of her hand and across the kitchen table before crashing down against the floor and shattering the ceramic squares underneath. She jumped as the crash boomed, spun to affirm Terry still lay lifeless and undisturbed, and then ran down the steps.

───────── ◆ ─────────

Once surrounded in silent darkness once again, Daisy tucked herself into the tightest ball she could, and wrapped her arms around her bony knees that rested against her chest. Her healthy weight of just a week ago would have prevented such a position, but now her body seemed to wither away, shrinking more and more through each passing day of starvation.

"Daisy."

Daisy raised her head at the whisper of her name, waiting to see if what she heard was real.

"Daisy," Samantha called out once more, her voice just above a whisper this time.

"Yeah?" She replied, looking up at the stairs for a sign of Uncle Terry, feeling both scared and confused.

"It's me, baby girl."

"Sammy?"

"Yes, baby. I'm here."

Daisy darted toward the sound of her sister's voice and tripped over her own feet that ran beneath her stiff legs, sending her skidding face down to where Sam sat waiting. "Sammy!" Daisy yelled, as she scrambled to her feet and fell into Sam's lap, sobbing into her chest as Sam lifted her shackled hands and wrapped her arms tightly around her shivering body.

"Shhh, baby. We have to keep quiet," she whispered, wiping away her own tears. "Shhh, Shhh, Shhh. It's okay my girl. It's going to be okay."

"I knew you would come for me," Daisy said through a tender smile, as she hugged her arms and legs around Sam's body, squeezing as hard as her weak body could manage. Just then they heard glass shatter against the floor, just above their heads, followed by Terry's bellowing voice and another loud thud, which seemed to shake the very foundation of the little house above.

"Go back to your spot, Daisy."

"But I don't want to," she cried back.

"You need to, sunshine. Right now, trust me."

Daisy listened to her sister, as always, and quickly returned to the blanket and resumed her fetal position, just as Uncle Terry had left her.

As soon as she was tucked around her knees once more, the door flew open and the light switched on. And Daisy threw up the bile from her twisted stomach, knowing exactly what she was now expected to do.

CHAPTER 38

As night settled around the station its doors suddenly flew open beneath Brody's angry thrust as he stormed through. He stomped his way to the conference room with equal impatience before centering his emotions as he walked through the door to join the meeting, already in progress.

"That was quick," said Special Agent Townsend. "Good man."

"What do we have?" Said Brody.

"The floor is yours, Rookie," replied Townsend.

"I think I found something in the file," he said, still feeling nervous and painfully green in front of the seasoned professionals he wished to soon become. "A letter Arlene wrote to Chad, dated four years ago, long after he was last seen," he continued as he held the letter in his hands.

"Read it," said Brody.

"Yes, sir."

My Dear Chad,

After all these years it seems my heart will not forget its love for you. Just goes to show how worthless a woman's heart can be, and how I must remain steadfast against its lying whispers of happiness. Love got me nowhere the first time around. Gave me nothing in return except your pity and hate. Made my mind lose control, taking you from me forever. Had me believing I could move on to a better man without you around.

But my heart lied. Made me suffer just as much as your refusal to love me did. I'm pregnant again, my love. Don't be mad though, the father is nothing compared to you, even weak and confused as you were. I told him I was expecting and he ran back to his wife and family,. Haven't been able to find him since. But I will find him my darling, and make him pay as you did. It is only fair. And once I do, I will come to you. You will be mine once more in the eternity of our after-life. The only place you cannot run away from.

Forever Yours,
Arlene.

"Good work, Rook. Doesn't shed a whole lot of light on the paternal father of Daisy, but I think it's enough to confirm the murder of Mr. Beckensworth, as we suspected," said Brody.

"And to connect it with Arlene," finished Townsend. "And if Arlene held true to her word, Daisy's father can, at this point, be assumed alive. Lucky man he was to run away when he did."

"And what of Jackson? Good information for the case against Arlene, but two little girls are still in the hands of a monster," replied Brody, quickly growing impatient.

"Agent Cooper is researching a few possible leads for a known address as we speak, said Townsend. "Nothing solid so far."

"Sit Brody," said the Lieutenant. "Lets go over and review what we know so far. The records we pulled which matched the serial number of the pre-paid phone had only one other number called before all activity suddenly ceased. We also pulled Jacksons phone records and found he dialed that same number as recently as two days ago."

"Please tell me you have already identified the owner of this number," replied Brody as he suddenly became hopeful once more.

"We have. It is a direct line belonging to the Westmire County Clerk's Office."

"The County Clerk's Office? Jesus Christ, LT., why didn't you start with that!"

"We have officers en route to interview every county employee with access to that line," the Lieutenant said reassuringly. "We called ahead and demanded all employees return to the office immediately, as most were already headed home."

"You know what this means, don't you. If Jackson has a connection on the inside of a government building, he has full access to everything he needs to make those girls completely disappear. Fake identification, fake birth certificates, even falsified passports."

"Exactly."

"He is taking them out of the country," said Brody with absolute certainty. "He said so himself. There's always some truth behind every lie, and he said—on record—he's taking his wife overseas for "treatment". We need to get into every international flight record, now."

"Of course, Brody. You're dead on," replied Townsend with equal urgency.

Just then, the door, which sealed in the rising tension of the conference room, flew open as Agent Cooper sped in. "We have it. An address on file from the Secretary of State for a Ms.

Angelica Palmer, updated just six months ago when she renewed her Drivers License.

"Go!" Demanded the Lieutenant. I will stay here and work the flight records."

But Brody and Townsend were already on their way out the door with Agent Cooper before he could finish his order. The three men piled themselves into Brody's car, the closest to the station doors, and sped heading south as Cooper entered the address into the GPS before securing it into the holster, already suctioned to the windshield.

"You will reach your destination in forty seven minutes," said the machine's womanly, robotic voice.

"Forty seven minutes my ass," said Brody in return as he gunned the gas pedal toward the highway, with several patrol cars keeping pace behind as their sirens wailed. The freeway had long since cleared from the bumper-to-bumper crawl of rush hour traffic, and the spattering of travelers that did remain, obeyed the racing convoy of flashing lights by efficiently removing themselves from obstruction.

They arrived in just under 30 minutes, and all men exited their cars immediately in calm order. Brody and Townsend took their place at the front door with two policemen steadily protecting their back, guns ready, while Cooper and the rest of the officers manned the back door and every window.

"Jackson!" Brody hollered as he pounded the door. "Open up!"

He turned the handle door and found it unlocked. With his gun in ready position, he kicked open the door and proceeded in. "Jackson!" He yelled once more as the rest of the crew followed in behind.

"Brody," said one of the officers. "Look here." He pointed to the inside door handle covered in tacky blood. And without saying a word the men pushed forward while bracing themselves for what possibly lay ahead. After spreading out and kicking open each closed door, they convened once again and entered the kitchen as one forceful unit, stopping as quickly as they had entered, as each took in the scene that displayed itself amongst the disheveled kitchen floor.

An open bottle of Brandy lay empty on its side atop the off-white table, its contents still slowly dripping into the bloody mixture of broken glass and smeared footprints below. "Is anybody here," Brody called out once more before heading down the stairs of the open cellar door.

He stopped at the bottom as Townsend followed, offering more light from his black, industrial flashlight. Brody went directly to Daisy's red bag to look inside and was immediately hit with the potent smell of urine as he dug through. He looked over at Townsend holding an orange doll made of yarn that had been left behind. "We missed them," he said. But Brody didn't respond, as his attention called him toward the open shackles chained and bolted into the concrete floor. Nor did he see Townsend open his suit jacket and secure the doll in the pocket beneath his chest.

"We need forensics here," he finally said as he held the shackle up towards Townsend with the end of his ballpoint pen, and pointed to the fresh blood inside with his sturdy index finger, strong and reliable like the branch of an old oak tree.

CHAPTER 39

"Daisy!" Shouted Angel. "Get up, we need to get out of here now!"

"Stay away from her!" Shouted Sam as she ran fast ahead before the chains length ran short, abruptly sending her face first into the cement.

"It's okay, Sammy. It's just Angel. She's nice," said Daisy as her hands flew up to cover her sweet little mouth. "Oops. I told our secret! But I can't keep no secrets from my Sammy."

Angel turned her attention toward Samantha. "I'm getting us out of here. Fuck!" She said in panic as she examined the locked shackles.

"I think he put the key in his pants pocket," Samantha answered. "I heard it drop and clang against something. Like loose change, maybe."

Angel hesitated for a moment before heading up the steps, two at a time, this time her pain non-existent through her pumping adrenaline. She reached first into Terry's left pocket only to find it empty, and then into his right, relieved as she pulled out a handful of cold metal. She opened her fist to find a single silver key, contrasted amongst several golden torpedo shaped bullets, reminding her that Terry was always armed and ready. She lifted his pant leg and snatched the gun he kept tethered to his ankle before running back down the steps.

Once Samantha was free, Angel quickly led the girls up and away from their captivity. "I don't want you to be afraid, Daisy," Angel said as they reached the top of the steps. "He can't hurt you now." Once through the door, however, Daisy was scared from the sight of the blood stained floor, and from Terry lying so dangerously close. She buried her face into Samantha as they were ushered out the back kitchen door.

"Wait right here," said Angel as she dashed back into the house and quickly returned with Terry's car keys and cell phone.

"Is he dead?" Sam asked.

"No, I don't think so," Angel answered, as she quickly opened the car door for the girls to climb in. "But he should be out for awhile." I hope so anyway, she thought. She pulled slowly from the driveway, trying to remain quiet to keep attention away from the horror inside of the house, speeding only once they were a few miles away, but far yet from safety.

"Where are we going?" Demanded Samantha from the back seat.

"I don't know yet. I haven't had time to think that through."

"Well we should call the police," Sam said.

"Don't you realize that Terry IS the police? It isn't safe to call them. It isn't safe to call anyone."

"I know somebody you can call. Detective Brody, he's that man's partner."

Angel laughed at Sam's ignorance in the rearview mirror. "Oh yeah, lets call HIM. We might as well just go back and wait for Terry to wake up and finish what he started."

"I mean it, Angel. I know him. You can trust him. He had nothing to do with this, and he is going to kill Terry himself once he finds out what he's done."

"I don't think so, kid. Not going to happen."

"Well when you come up with a better plan, just let me know," said Sam sarcastically, irritated by the way Angel had called her a kid. She hugged into Daisy, thankful she was again in her arms.

Angel drove for two hours in silence, unable to formulate a reasonable plan with no form of identification and no money in her wallet. Panic began to set in as she looked at the gas gauge with only a quarter tank remaining. "God help me," she whispered. Then, as she looked forward, she saw a sign to the right of the highway detailing a State Park just ahead at the next exit, and she found her answer.

As she turned into the park and drove around the closed barrier of the after-hours gate, she looked back at the girls sound asleep in each other's arms, confirming to her heart that she had done the right thing. She drove down the narrow winding road that led deep into the park until she found a spot, as good as any, to rest and think of her next step.

———— ◆ ————

Terry came-to and remained stiff and still along the kitchen floor, blinking his eyes in confusion as he saw his own pool of blood next to where is head lay throbbing in pain. He slowly hoisted himself on all fours and screamed Angel's name, realizing she was gone and that she had taken the girls as he focused on the small footprints left scattered in his blood. He heaved himself to his feet, dragging them through the dead weight of his legs toward the kitchen table. He knocked over the bottle of Brandy in anger from the absence of his phone, before continuing towards his bedroom, weaving in and out of blackness as he pushed himself slowly forward.

He woke up again to the spinning of his head, this time with his face planted into the berber carpet of his room, just in front of his oak dresser drawers. He pulled open the bottom drawer and used it to shoulder some of his weight as he rose to his feet once more, determined to get to Angel before she ran too far away. After steadying himself for just a moment against the dresser's sturdy weight, he opened his pinewood box and retrieved his in-case-of-emergency phone, flipped it open, and dialed the number with his thin, bloody thumb.

"Yeah," said the man on the other end.

"It's Jackson. I need your help."

"Jackson," said the man flatly. "Glad you called. I had some visitors this evening. At the office. They are on to you, buddy. And if this gets traced back to me, you're fucking dead."

"Don't you threaten me, boy. You want this cleaned up, you get here now. Angel left and took the kids. Now come get me, and you can help finish them off yourself. Or don't, and I will fucking hunt you down, and kill you personally," said Terry before flipping the phone shut to end the call, further resonating his threatening demand of obedience.

Terry laid his back over the side of his bed while his feet remained planted on the floor, still fighting against the swirling darkness edging in and out of his furious consciousness. Twenty minutes later his front door opened and Terry smiled with the satisfaction of his triumph, of his own superior power to rule any man's will, as he so desired.

"Lets go," said the man, his face obscured in mystery beneath the shifting shadows of the dark house.

"We finally meet," said Terry.

"Fuck the pleasantries and let's go."

Terry raised himself from the bed while deliberately keeping his cool, letting this man believe he had a momentary upper hand. His lips twisted with the anticipation of fear he would soon induce, once his body was again able.

"Christ, Jackson. You let that woman do a number on you good," laughed the man with absolute amusement as he looked ahead at the all-powerful-Jackson, reduced to a staggering weakling at the hands of his own woman.

"She drugged me. Not good enough though. Carry this," said Jackson as he handed the man his canvas black bag with his laptop, the passports, a gun and ammunition inside. "We can track her through my phone—she took it with her. As soon as she makes a call, if she hasn't already, she's ours."

"Can't wait," the man replied as he followed towards the living room and out the front door.

The men wasted no time and headed out in a brand-new red F150, the man behind the wheel, and Terry with his laptop ready in the passenger seat. They drove to the closest interstate and headed south by intuition alone, stopping at every exit and gas station along the way to ask if the trio had been seen.

Twenty minutes into the ride Jackson began to feel the fog loosen and rise just slightly from its heavy blanket around his mind. "What's your name, stranger?" Jackson asked.

"You can call me Roger."

"Roger, that," mocked Jackson in return. "Any GPS activity yet?"

"No. Dumb bitch. She's probably waiting till she's far enough away to feel safe first, if she makes a call at all. She has nobody, no friends or family, and, thanks to, me trusts nobody either. I'm sure one of the brats will talk her into reaching out to somebody before too long, weak and stupid as she is."

"Hope so," returned Roger.

Jackson knew from their phone conversations that this man, Roger, was one of few words, which suited him just fine. All he cared about was that he kept his word, and delivered his documents on time. Absolute efficiency was the only way Jackson could work, and would settle for nothing less from a partner in return. As leery as he was to work with someone new, he trusted the recommendation of his counterpart in Vegas, the head ringleader of the Strips Human Trafficking Trade, and the one who introduced him into the business (while simultaneously working the case against his new friend with the Las Vegas Police Department).

"Think we should stay put at the next exit?" Asked Roger. "Don't want to waste time by hunting in the wrong direction."

"She went south. It's the quickest way to cross state lines. We keep going," Jackson said matter-of-factly.

"You're the boss. It's your ass, after all."

As the F150 barreled onto the onramp after another dead end interview, Jackson's laptop lit up as a GPS ping rang into the truck's cabin.

"She's making a call."

CHAPTER 40

Brody gathered Townsend and Cooper together with two officers he had hand picked from the team-in-blue once the forensic army arrived to take over the scene. Brody knew they did not have time to wait for the evidence to be processed if he was to get to the girls in time. Even if forensics worked through the night in the lab, he was afraid it would still be too late. In fact, he was afraid the girls were already in the air headed to only god-knows-where, lost away in the vast possibilities the other side of the Ocean offered a man like Jackson.

"I think our best option is to set up shop in Ms. Chandler's home," said Brody.

"Ms. Chandler's home?" replied Cooper.

"Yes. Ms. Chandler and myself are the only people Samantha knows, the only people she trusts. It may work to our advantage, her being taken into Jackson's ring. She is smart beyond her years. A survivor. And if she has the opportunity to call, she will call."

"And you are sure she will call one of you, and not directly to the station, or 911 for that matter?" Asked Agent Cooper.

"Positive. She will call me, I'm sure of it. And if not, we will have Ms. Chandlers phone tapped as well, it's likely the only other number she knows."

"Lets get to it," said Townsend. "Makes the most sense to me."

Brody phoned Carly on the way to fill her in on the plan, and what developments had taken place since he left her sitting alone and dazed many hours before. Once the team arrived they immediately went to work, hooking up both phones to the tracking equipment, which not only recorded the conversation, but tracked the caller's exact location within minutes of a connected line. Carly put on a fresh pot of coffee and filled her silver serving tray with cream, sugar and fresh cinnamon rolls she had picked up from the bakery early that morning. She carried her offerings to the kitchen table surrounded by grateful men with empty stomachs.

"Fresh and hot," Carly said before joining Brody who stood against the butter yellow molding of the kitchen's grand entrance. Both resisted the urge to embrace their hands, which hung so close together that each could feel the heat smoldering out from the other. Carly and Brody were fully aware of the new tension building in the air between them, but were too fully engaged in the anticipation which grew stronger as each minute of the cruel waiting game passed them by.

"This waiting is killing me," Carly finally said. "I am not cut out for this at all."

"Waiting is indeed the toughest part. But at this hour of night, nothing more we can do but wait and hope," said Townsend with his reassuring and reasonable tone. And both his confident voice and silvered hair of experience did, indeed, reassure her jittering anxiety. Just a bit.

"Wait and hope," Carly repeated.

"Why don't you lay down and rest on the couch. It's getting really late and this could go on until morning. I will have an officer wake you the second a call comes in," said Brody, desperate to ease Carly's worry.

"No way. Rest isn't an option for me right now, even if I wanted it," she responded with conviction.

"I know," said Brody as his hand met hers in a tender squeeze, which was noticed and processed immediately by Townsend. "It was just a thought," he said with one more hug of his hand, before releasing himself from her in response to the expression on Townsend's disapproving face. Carly moved away to refill the empty cups and replenish the pot with a fresh brew to keep the men alert.

"Brody, a word please."

"Yes, sir," he responded as he followed Townsend into the sitting room, and away from the rest of the crew and their curious ears.

"Is something going on with you and Ms. Chandler?" Townsend demanded through his subtle but succinct tone.

"No, however, it would be irrelevant to you or anyone if there was," Brody replied back in agitation. He was confused enough as it was about his feelings for Carly, trying to justify or explain them was not only offensive, but impossible as well.

"Let me ask in a different way. Are you too close to this case? Tell me now and tell me honestly. You are the best of the best, Brody, an elite in our field, and you know damn well what can happen to an investigation when personal feelings meddle their way in. They can corrupt and blur what is ethical, can compromise clear and concise action, and can put the safety of the ones involved in serious danger."

"I know that, Agent. And I am not too close, I can promise you that. I have, of course, become quite fond of Samantha, smitten actually. And I admire Ms. Chandler for what she has done for that little girl, for her compassion to heal Samantha and offer her a better life. And that is where it ends."

Townsend looked into Brody's eyes in silence for several seconds. "You love her," he finally said.

"Jesus Christ, man! You—"

Townsend held up his hand to halt Brody's upcoming rant. "It is my job to read people, to know what is in their heads even when they can not, or will not, say it too themselves. And I am damn good at my job. I may be old, detective, but my senses are sharp as ever."

"Well you have it wrong this time, sir. Dead wrong," Brody countered through his sudden steely green eyes. "I lost my love and my only child a long time ago, before my boy had even entered the world to take his first breath.

267

Neither survived through childbirth, and love is something I will never do again. Not like that."

"I'm sorry for your loss. Truly sorry. But, respectfully, I am not dead wrong, I'm afraid. And you, too, will realize so when this is all over. You're a good man, Brody. And you deserve a woman like the one waiting in the kitchen. Just keep the lid on tight until the case is closed, you hear?"

"There is no lid, but yes. I hear you," Brody replied to himself, as Townsend had already left the room.

———————— ◆ ————————

Samantha lay stretched out along the back seat with her Daisy sleeping peacefully, for the first time in over a week, in the warmth of their bodies spooned tightly together. Sam had been awake for some time but remained still, waiting for Angel to finally succumb to the unavoidable demand of sleep. She stared at the back of Angel's head for ten full minutes as she studied the different shades of her hair. It started with an inch of black which grew fresh from her scalp, followed by two inches of bright gold contrasting against her dark roots like a single gold nugget trying to hide amongst a pile of coal. The gold seemed to blend into the next layer of copper, ending where the bright white of bleach began, just below her ears. So different from the soft honey blonde of Ms. Chandler, she thought.

Once Sam was thoroughly sure Angel was deep in sleep, she gingerly lifted herself up using the back of the seat for support, careful not to jostle Daisy out of her own sleeping security. She reached up and slowly slid the phone off of the center console and hid it in the waistband of her jeans and beneath her shirt. She tried to unlock her door manually with her fingertips; not wanting to risk the loud click of the power locks ruining her only chance to call out to Brody. The nub of the lock was small and smooth, and depressed so far down that her fingers kept sliding off as it stay stubbornly in place. She used her slender pinky fingers on both hands to reach down as deep as she could and applied direct pressure on each side, shimmying it back and forth slowly until it finally popped up into her unlocked freedom.

Sam paused a moment before slowly pulling the handle open, making just a slight pop as the door released. She crawled out the door and remained crouched down on her hands and knees as she guided the open door back to the car, leaving it slightly ajar in the name of keeping quiet. She crawled herself behind the back tires and towards a grassy bank which lay in front of a thick wooded area, perfect for providing privacy. She looked towards the car, still motionless and sleeping, and dialed Brody's number as her pulse raced through her veins.

She waited for the sweet sound of the ring to meet her ear, but heard only silence, followed by the quick beep of a bad connection. She looked down at the phone and read 'searching for service' on the display, and nearly screamed out in frustration. She walked herself out from the obstruction of the woods until a single signal bar lit up in response. She dialed again, this time a successful ring filled her eager ear. One ring, two, and then three as her heart began to sink.

———— ◆ ————

Brody kept his distance from Carly following Townsend's presumptive accusations, and planted himself at the kitchen table, a cup of coffee a constant in the grip of his hands. Conversation around him flowed in and right back out of his ears as the officers to his right were passing the time with an intense game of five card poker. Townsend and Cooper had set up shop in the small living room adjacent to the kitchen, keeping the men both in seclusion from distraction, and in close proximity to the central hub should quick action be required. They used their federal resources to continue on the investigation through the obstruction of the night hour, focused mainly on the research of all passengers booked for every upcoming international flight.

Carly, too, kept herself occupied by penning her heartache and hopes into the pages of her journal, as she sat in front of the soft glowing comfort Brody had prepared in the fireplace to help calm her racing mind. She argued against it at first, not wanting him to go to such trouble. But once she sat mesmerized in the fire's crackling flames, a comfort washed over her indeed, as the warm distraction soothed her severed nerves.

A gradual silence blanketed through each room. A sudden calm rolled slowly into each corner of the house just before the shrill ring of Brody's phone sent them all jumping to their feet, all instantly alert, as they rushed together around the kitchen table. Brody snatched the phone in his hand, holding back his rush to answer until the machine clicked on and the tape began to roll.

"Hello!"

Only silence returned his plea. "Hello!" He called out once more. Then he heard the beep of the disconnected call.

"God DAMMIT!"

———— ◆ ————

Just as Sam heard the deep comfort of Brody's voice, the phone beeped loudly indicating the signal had been lost, the call unforgivingly cut from the unsecured air. She now had no choice but to completely exit the woods and risk her voice carrying through the clear air and into the open car door. She crawled herself down into the grassy bank and lay flat on her stomach to provide full obscurity from the small hill above. She dialed again, this time through a two bar signal, and prayed the call would hold through long enough to get help.

She sat through each rhythmic tone once more as the pause between each ring seemed to brutally expand its lengthy silence, one by one, until finally she again heard the strong voice of her waiting rescuer.

———— ◆ ————

The men stayed standing in complete silence, staring at the phone Brody had just slammed onto the unsuspecting table, before Carly spoke up. "What happened?" She asked.

"Dead air," Brody said.

"Could it have been them?" Carly pleaded.

"Could be, the connection didn't stand long enough to tell."

"Well shouldn't you call back?" Carly demanded, aware Brody knew what to do, yet unable to hold back her emotions which made her feel helpless and small.

Brody remained stoically still until his phone rang through the room a second time. "Hello," he said once the recorder clicked back to life, this time keeping his voice completely reserved.

Just as the Federal Agents secured their headphones in place to listen in, Samantha's sweet voice answered their hopeful curiosity in a soft-spoken whisper.

"Detective Brody. It's Samantha Beckett. I need your help."

"Where are you," answered Brody, as he signaled a thumbs up to the rest of the team, confirming the eagerness displayed across their waiting faces.

"I don't know, some kind of woodsy place."

"Tell me exactly what you see and be as specific as you can," Brody said calmly.

"We drove around a gate to get in because the place is closed. We passed lots of trails and a few old buildings, but it is so dark here I could hardly see. We drove for a while and passed a long stretch with no trees, and I could see a big lake from my window. I couldn't tell it was a lake at first, until I saw the reflection of the moon, kind of like it was floating on top of the water."

"Keep going, Sam. You are doing excellent."

"We are back in the dark now but I can still see some light glowing from the moon, it's really big and full tonight. We aren't too far from the lake, though. We only drove for a minute or so after I saw it. Angel parked to rest just in front of an old playground."

"Angel," said Brody. "Who else are you with?"

"Just her and Daisy. Brody, I have my Daisy," she replied, as she choked back a sudden wave of tears that emerged from the happiness of confirming her sister's whereabouts out loud. "Your partner, the one that came to Ms. Chandler's house, is the one who took us," she finished.

"We know, hon. Where is he right now?"

"I don't know, still at his house I hope. Angel drugged him and knocked in his head with a frying pan to get us out of there, but she is convinced he is already out looking for us. Please hurry and find us. Please," she emphasized through her desperate whisper.

Brody looked over to Townsend to see if they secured their location yet, and he shook his head no in response. "I need you to stay on the phone, Sam. Don't hang up until I tell you to, okay? It's sounds like you are in a state park somewhere. Can you tell me how long Angel drove until she stopped there?"

"A long time, a couple hours maybe. Oh! And I noticed just as we got off the freeway that we were driving south, if that helps."

Townsend lifted the right side of his headphone from his ear, "We got it," he said, and Brody nodded his head forward in affirmation.

"We have your location, Sam. You did good. Really good. We have police officers dispatched and they are on their way. It is going to be a little while until they arrive, though, and I need you to promise me you will stay safe, and do whatever it takes to stay put until we get there."

"You're coming too, right?"

"I'm already on my way. See you soon."

CHAPTER 41

"They are south, indeed," laughed Jackson. "Just under an hour away."

"I will get us there in half that," said Roger. "Just tell me the way."

"Straight ahead. So fucking predictable. Keep going to exit 66. They are just off the highway hiding out in Mayfield State Park."

"Superb," said Roger, " and isolated."

As the truck barreled ahead in a blur of bright red, Roger contemplated sharing the irony of their current situation with Jackson, for no other reason than momentary entertainment to pass the time. After all, once they rid themselves of the sharp thorns, which threatened to pierce through the safe bubble of the men's freedom,

Jackson, too, would meet his end from the hands of Roger himself. It was the only way to burn every last loose thread connecting him to his secret life of crime.

"Want to hear something wild?" Asked Roger.

"Why not," said Jackson in return.

"Get ready to have your mind blown. So when you first called me requesting the falsified passports for the two girls, I thought nothing of it. Thought it was routine, business as usual. But I had to cross reference their legal names to ensure no other government documents existed in the database which could be traced back to their unique fingerprints, and back to me."

"Yeah," said Jackson. "And your point?"

"I thought the name Beckett sounded familiar but couldn't pinpoint why. So I ran a search on their mother," he laughed.

"And?"

"And," he repeated with emphasis, "I knew the woman staring back at me from the computer screen. I knew her very well," he laughed in cocky satisfaction. "She was a piece of trash I fucked on the side, years ago."

"No way," said Jackson in enthusiastic surprise.

"Seriously. Bitch got pregnant too, tried to pin it on me. Shit, might have been mine for all I know, but there was no way I was getting tied up in that train wreck for the rest of my life. Thankfully she never knew my real name. She was too hungry for my money to see past the bull shit I fed her, she slurped it right up."

"So the young one might be yours and you sold her out anyway? Jesus, and I thought I was a son-of-a-bitch."

"Might be. No matter to me either way. I'm not in the business of turning away good, easy money. Especially not for some bastard child of a worthless whore."

The two men hollered out with pleasure in unison, their laughter sealed together with the dark evil of their black souls. Roger was right, his little ditty distracted them so thoroughly with their shared superiority that they almost missed the exit, as the truck swerved over to the right just in time to drive up the ramp and into the waiting park ahead.

Roger slowed the truck as they drove down the winding road guided by the blinking dot pulsing from Jackson's computer screen. Once passed the glassy lake, he slowed even more, careful not to make the slightest sound to alert the girls who waited out in the vulnerable open, like lost little calves trapped in a circle of bloodthirsty wolves.

"There," said Jackson, as the headlights illuminated the parked car, its sleek black paint bouncing the light right back at them.

Roger flipped off his bright beams as the truck eerily crunched toward their prey through the parking lot made of dirt and stones. Samantha heard someone approaching and shot up in absolute relief.

"That was fast!" She said with excitement. "Angel, wake up. Help is here!"

Angel awoke abruptly. "What did you do!" She screamed.

"It's okay. I called Detective Brody to come save us. It was the only way."

Just then, a furious fist pounded into the driver side window. Angel turned her head to meet the barrel of Terry's gun pointed straight at her, separated from her face by the thin window glass, just as weak as her own shaking body. She turned to Samantha before opening the car door. "You can trust him, huh? You better hug your sister goodbye one last time," she said, before surrendering herself into Terry's murderous grip. He yanked her out of the car before he stuck his head into the back seat, telling the girls if they wanted to stay alive they had better stay put.

They shook violently in each others arms, terrified further by the spit and foam that accompanied Terry's threatening scowl. He and Roger dragged Angels writhing body away from the car and into the ditch behind, as she pleaded for her underserved forgiveness, which fell completely deaf upon their emotionless ears.

They took turns beating her until she could no longer feel her body in pain, and waited to finally be free in the arms of death, which teased her with its promise of relief, only to release her once more into the torture of endless punishment. Angel felt Terry slide her jeans from her limp and lifeless legs before he ripped away the black lace beneath, leaving her fully exposed as he called her a whore.

"Have at it," Terry said, as he walked backward, offering Roger the pleasure of his property. He kept his eyes fixed on Angel's body as it was roughly thrust up and down beneath the body of a complete stranger. "Like riding a horse, isn't it, love" Terry taunted, as he grew hard with the lust of his absolute and dominating power.

With the men's attention fully occupied, Samantha led Daisy from the car knowing it was the only chance at keeping them safe, knowing that Brody was trustworthy no matter what Angel said, and knowing wholeheartedly that he was still on his way. She needed to find a hiding spot to buy them some time until he arrived, but was unable to see far enough ahead in the dead dark of the night sky.

"Faster!" Sam said as she dragged Daisy by the hand, running straight ahead into the park and past the swings, that, during the day, offered children like them nothing but simple and carefree joy. "Hurry, baby," she whispered as they crossed to the other side, far away from the monkey bars and twirling slide, and into the deep dark woods, which crunched beneath their nervous little feet. "Use your tip-toes, baby girl. Be as quiet as a sweet little mouse."

CHAPTER 42

Special Agent Townsend attached the magnetic siren to the top of Brody's car as it squealed away from Carly's house and barreled ahead through every red light, while Cooper navigated their destination from the back seat. Brody floored the engine as soon as his wheels passed over the on-ramp and into the fluidity of the freeway ahead, pushing his speed to the car's absolute limit, passing the wailing screams of the cruisers already in route.

The distance separating the rescue squad from the victims was a race against the light of the morning hours, until a call came through, making the little window of time they had thoroughly non-existent.

"Lieutenant here. We have new activity coming from the prepaid phone. A single call out to an unknown number. A search of the entire perimeter of the Jackson home came back clear, and a neighbor saw a red truck arrive in the driveway sometime around 1 am. It is likely Jackson phoned for help and has a partner with him as we speak."

"Got it," said Brody, as he willed his car faster with the inertia of his determination and the weight of his heavy foot, knowing he was now fighting against the conclusive reality that the children remained Jackson's hunted prey.

———◆———

Roger recoiled his body back from between Angel's legs just in time for his demonic deed to pulsate from his body onto the ground below, just beside Angel's lifeless feet. He gathered dried leaves and branches to cover atop his spilled desire, and lit the pile in flames to burn away the evidence he left behind. "You gonna have a go?" He said to Jackson, still grinning toward the scene ahead.

"No time," he replied just before he fired a single shot into Angel's bloodied head. A tiny scream yelped out in the far distance in reaction the sudden bang, which echoed through the dark silence, straight across the park, and into the petrified ears of the hiding girls.

"Looks like they ran," said Roger, as both men gazed in the direction of the scream.

"Not surprised. Let's go get 'em," Jackson replied through his growing irritation.

"Don't sound so down, man. Might as well enjoy the thrill of the chase since we have no choice anyway. Will make taking them out much more satisfying."

"We're not taking them out."

"Excuse me?" Roger slowly enunciated, as he stopped Jackson mid-stride and shoved his body with both hands to angle it in front of his own.

"Don't fucking touch me," Jackson spit out in return. "You think I'm going to kill my investment? Let over six figures of profit just bleed out in these goddamned woods?"

"And what do I get out of the deal, then?" Asked Roger as the patience of his rage wore murderously thin.

"What do you get? How about your freedom?" Jackson replied. "Don't worry, your name is clear, and by this afternoon I will be on a flight to Thailand with the girls by their "loving daddy's" side, and you will never hear from me again."

"It's too big a risk, Jackson. Have you lost your mind?"

"I have no choice. I can't run away from this. Not now. I have to leave the country and never return. That bitch left me no other choice. And I'll be damned if I don't salvage my reputation in the meantime. If I show up empty handed, I can kiss any life I need to make for myself abroad goodbye."

Jackson contemplated just killing Roger now. He was growing tired of his elitist bullshit attitude, and wasting the little dark that remained by demanding justification for his actions, which were none of Roger's business. But he decided he would rather use the second set of eyes and ears to his fullest advantage, before giving in to the pleasure of watching Roger's stunned face as he drifted away into the darkness of his own death.

Roger, too, held back his urge to grab for the small pistol strapped to his ankle beneath his pants, and just finish Jackson now. But he also needed help to locate the hiding girls before the exposing sun rose in the sky, bringing the park back to life with its warming light. "I get it," Roger said. "Let's get this over with so I can get the hell out of here."

The two men called out to the girls as they looked in every slide, play cove, and jungle gym, until every hiding spot the playground offered came up empty. "The woods," Jackson pointed. "They can't be far." They stopped every few steps to listen for the crunching sound of retreat from beneath the shoes of their trapped victims.

"They aren't moving," said Roger. "They are either hiding in here somewhere, or long gone."

"Shhh. Listen."

Both men smiled in the black shield of the woods as they heard the faint hum of a song flutter sweetly through the trees above, just a short distance away. As they followed the lullaby of reassurance from one sister to the other, a twig snapped under the shoe of the hunter, bringing instant silence into the thicket once more. All four bodies remained still, each pair waiting for the other to move first. Roger then brought the surrounding space into vision with the illuminating light from his phone.

"There," Jackson pointed his finger, leading Roger's gaze to an enormous hollowed out log, which lay camouflaged against the fresh spring ground under years of built-up, spongy moss. They walked over and crouched down, shining the phone's light onto the quivering faces of the two girls who faced their absolute terror staring back in return.

"Get out," said Terry, and the girls obeyed.

"Please, don't hurt Daisy," Samantha pleaded. "I made her leave the car with me. It's my fault."

The two men just laughed in response as they separated the girls from one another and led them back to the waiting vehicles ahead. Once there, Jackson and Terry opened the back seat doors on each side, and simultaneously threw the girls in, sending their heads crashing into one another as they landed against the slippery leather. Both doors slammed shut and Roger headed around the car toward Jackson, as the soft glow of morning lit up the darkening of his eyes, and the pistol in his hand.

Jackson lunged forward into Roger's chest, which toppled the men into the rocky dust below as they rolled around, each trying to obtain the upper hand as they feverishly clawed at one another for ultimate control. Jackson's demonic strength soon gained total power as he straddled his weight on top of his prize, thrusting furious punches into Roger's bloody face. He put down his gun to retrieve Roger's own discarded pistol, to further insult his ultimate defeat. Jackson looked straight into Roger's eyes as he jammed the metal barrel into the center of his forehead, and laughed just before splattering Roger's head in two with a single bullet from his very own gun.

Samantha and Daisy looked out from the car window to witness the whole scene, unable to peel their paralyzed gaze away, even though they wanted desperately to do so. "Uncle Terry is coming!" Daisy cried out as he stormed toward the car.

"Get out," demanded Jackson as he ripped open the car door.

"We are going to be okay," Samantha lied, in a hopeless attempt to quiet Daisy's heavy sobs. "I'm here baby, right here."

Jackson gripped both girls around the back of their necks and led them into the backseat of the pick-up, newly freed from its previous owner. He slammed himself into the driver's seat and peeled away, reaching the highway just as the dust settled back to the ground, and around the murdered bodies he left behind.

———— ◆ ————

Brody and his team were the first to arrive on scene as the car sped recklessly ahead. That is until Brody saw the body of a dead man laying face up, his head blown away in a glistening pool of red blood, shining deeply bright under the rising morning sun. He slammed his brakes, sending the car skidding in a complete circle atop the unsteady dirt road in equal response.

"Son of a BITCH," Brody screamed, as all three men flew out the doors and to their feet once the car came to a dusty stop. "Samantha!" He called out into the park's serenity, peaceful still despite the spilled blood, which soiled the ground of Mother Nature's beauty. But Brody already knew he was too late as he inspected Jackson's car, back doors still ajar, left purposely behind.

"Come look at this," called Cooper as he stood over Angel's dead and beaten body.

But Brody ignored the order and instead ran straight back into his parked car, fired the engine back to life, and slammed the gas pedal flat against the floor until the spinning tires gripped into the dirt and propelled the car forward. He flew past the arriving officers on his way out of the park, and motioned to them from out his window to keep heading in their current direction.

He knew where Jackson was headed, and would not waste a single second of the girls' lives by planning out the next plan of action with the others. He reacted with nothing less than the absolute haste the girls safety required, calling

Townsend only once many miles had passed behind.

"Did you find anything in the flight records?" Brody demanded right away.

"A few things," Townsend responded. "Agent Cooper and I are right behind you in a squad car. We left the park in the hands of your deputies, our influence will be needed with you at the airport," he finished.

"Good. Of course, that makes sense," Brody said, realizing he would, indeed, get much further with the Agents by his side.

"Don't be too hasty, Detective. I told you. You're too close. From here on out you wait for my direct orders, is that clear?"

"Sir." Brody confirmed.

"There is a family of four that booked a one way ticket to Thailand, a man and woman with two children close to our girls age. That is where our attention was focused before Samantha's call came in, and it's the most promising lead. The tickets are booked under the last name Weston, and the flight, number 632, is scheduled to take off this morning at 7:20 am ."

"Got it," said Brody.

"When you get there, you are to go straight to the international flight gates and wait for us to arrive at the front door. Cooper is phoning in now to demand the delay of all international departures until we arrive."

"Yes, sir," he said, before he whipped his phone into the passenger side door, sending it thudding into the seat below.

CHAPTER 43

Jackson kept his intimidating stare locked on the girls from the rearview mirror. He glanced ahead to the open road, and then straight back to them, amused by their scare-stricken faces as they clung tightly around one another. "Look over there," he said, as he exited the truck just slightly right onto the airport service drive, surrounded immediately by the roar of jet engines as they ascended majestically into the clear, blue sky. "Ever been on a plane?" He asked, keeping his tone softly opposite of the monstrous expression on his face.

Samantha shook her head no, while Daisy buried her face into her sisters beating chest.

"No?" Said Jackson. "How about you, little one? Aww, don't be like that, now," he said in response to Daisy's silent tremors as they escalated into weak, weeping convulsions of terror. "Don't be scared now," he continued, knowing he must at once calm their nerves and gain just a stitch of trust if he had any chance of boarding the flight without notice.

"Where are we going?" Asked Samantha, braving her own panic through her steadfast voice, knowing that she, too, must gain his trust in order to formulate a plan of their escape.

"We are off to a place with soft, sandy beaches that flow into an endless, deep blue sea. Where mysterious caves graced with emerald water hide deep in the jungle, waiting for us to discover their beauty. Where the sun shines down from the absolute heavens above, and onto a land filled with boundless beauty as far as your big eyes can see. My girls, we are heading to a place rich with opportunity and culture which can not be offered anywhere else in the world, I can guarantee."

He paused his speech as he saw Daisy's head raise from its burrow to look ahead, her eyes wide with wonder. Easier than I thought, he said to himself. Sam, however, was not as easily impressed.

"Don't you get it, girls? The hard part is over. No more cellar. Not ever again. Uncle Terry is so proud of you, little one. You did just as I told you to do, and in return you got your big sister back and a whole new life that waits ahead."

"But why," asked Samantha. "Why are you taking us with you?"

"All that my dear Angel and I ever wanted were children of our own, but she was ruined from the years she spent disrespecting her own body before I rescued her—just like I rescued the two of you. When I met your mother and discovered how eager she was to free herself, I knew you girls belonged with me, and that I would finally give Angel the answer to her prayers."

"Where is Ms. Angel?" Daisy sheepishly asked.

"That is the saddest part. She decided she didn't want you guys after all. But don't worry, not for one second. Uncle Terry is all you need, and I am sure I will find you a nice new mommy before too long," Jackson replied.

Daisy, with her sheer sweetness and resilient heart, still young enough to accept hope from the very man whom revealed to her the darkest side of humanity, began to feel the tight knots in her stomach release from around the heavy weight of her pure dread. Samantha played along as well. She loosened her own body language and hardened face in order to strategically play their captor's sick game of wit, and, above all, for her Daisy's piece of mind.

"The beaches, Sammy. Like we always dreamed of," Daisy said with pure enthusiasm.

"I know, baby girl. Exactly like we always dreamed of," Sam replied tenderly.

Jackson paid the toll and parked the cumbersome truck in the parking lot designated for long-term travelers. He clicked his body free from the restraint of his seat belt and turned toward the girls. "We have to go over some important things first," he said. "I am friends with every single person inside the airport, even the pilots. And especially the flight attendants. They told me we must fly away to our paradise under special names, you understand?"

"Sure," said Sam, pushing a youthful naiveté through her voice, fully hiding the actual resentment resonating in her head. "Sounds like fun, huh Daisy? Just like our make-believe stories."

"Take a good look at these," said Jackson as he handed back the passports for review. "I can't be your Uncle Terry in there. I am your Daddy because children are only allowed to fly to another country with their Daddy's. And we must follow all of their rules, right?"

"Right!" Daisy confirmed.

"Good girl. Our last name is Weston. Practice it out-loud."

"Weston," the girls voiced in unison.

"Again," Jackson demanded, and the girls, without objection, obeyed. "You," he pointed to Sam, "are now Julie. Julie Weston. And your sister is Ruth. Little Ruthie Weston. And you are only to refer to me as Dad from now on. Can you both manage that?"

"I think so," said Samantha.

"I think so isn't good enough. You must. If you break character, even just once, the air marshal, that's the airport police," he explained, "will snatch you away from me and send you straight to jail. And not just any jail, either. They will throw you right into the same cold cell as your mother so she can beat you, all day and all night. That will be your punishment for disobeying their extremely important rules."

Bullshit, Samantha said in her head. Absolute nonsense, she thought, as she confirmed out loud what was expected of them. "We understand. Don't we, Ruthie," she added for good measure, as she winked at her sister with a smile on her face.

"Excellent. Now let's head out."

The newly formed trio entered the airport and stood in the long line to check in and receive the boarding passes to Jackson's waiting riches and glorious escape, when he suddenly realized the obvious absence of a very key piece to his success. As the line moved efficiently forward, he scrambled for a reasonable excuse for their unreasonable absence of luggage. Especially for such an expansive, one-way trip.

"Good morning," Jackson greeted to the fat, surly woman behind the desk, as charm oozed thickly from his upbeat voice.

"Good morning, Mr. Weston," she returned as she looked at the flight vouchers and entered the information into the system, her fingers flying over the keyboard in a flurry of constant clicks from years of repetitive and mind-deadening practice. "Identification and passports, please."

"Of course. Here you go, Summer," said Jackson through a full smile as he read her name tag out loud. She met his smile and cracked a small one of her own.

"I see you booked a total of four passengers," she said as she pushed through the process without peeling her eyes from her computer screen as she worked.

"Yes, my wife was supposed to travel with us as well. She unfortunately is home sick as a dog with the flu, the poor thing. She didn't feel well enough to leave the house this morning, and we wouldn't want to get other vacation travelers sick anyway. We will need to change her flight to next week, but I will let her take care of that once she is feeling up to it."

"I see," said the clerk. "And how many bags will you be checking?" She asked, this time looking up, and then rising to look suspiciously down at the empty floor where their luggage should have been.

"This is why men shouldn't travel alone," Jackson laughed. "I rushed around all morning to get my wife stocked up with cold medicine and forgot our luggage in our living room. Sitting right beside the front door!" He emphasized, as he feigned embarrassment by momentarily hiding his eyes beneath his sweating palm. "We are staying with my wife's family, though. They will have all the essentials we need. Plus I have already called home, and Mrs. Weston will send our things just as soon as she can leave the bed."

"I see," the woman said once more, hesitating slightly before dismissing the small whisper of something awry, and handed Jackson his tickets of freedom. "Have a nice flight," she said in conclusion of her mandated script.

"And you have a nice day as well, ma'am," Jackson returned, as he grabbed both girls by each of their nervous hands and led them toward the boarding gate. "Good job," he said once they were through security, and checked in for a second time in the waiting area of their scheduled flight. The girls had remained obedient and silent the entire time, and smiled back at the appropriate times to each official who greeted them warmly as they passed through each stop.

"I have to go potty," Daisy finally said, unable to hold it anymore.

"Can I take her?" Samantha asked, praying he would allow her to.

"It will have to wait until we board," he answered matter-of-factly, leaving no room for further discussion on the subject.

"Yes sir," Samantha said.

"I can take her," said an elderly woman, as she swiveled around in her chair to meet Jackson's gaze. "I couldn't help but overhear. I certainly wouldn't want my children out of my sight either in this day and age," she continued, hoping the grey bun pinned high atop her head, along with the matronly ensemble of a trustworthy old woman would ease the worry of a protective father. There was just something in the little girl's voice that pleaded for help, and she selfishly needed to ease her own sudden worry.

"Thank you kindly," Jackson replied. "But I don't want you to go to any trouble. Look," he said as he pointed to the departure time digitally displayed in red against the far wall, "they should begin boarding in five minutes. You can wait, can't you, Ruthie?"

"Yes, Dad," Daisy replied through her welling eyes, as she squirmed uncontrollably in her seat from the pain of her throbbing bladder.

"That child is going to lose control," said the kind woman. "Just look at her."

"You have to go that bad, sweetie?" Jackson asked.

"Uh-huh," Daisy eagerly replied.

"Alrighty then. Thank you very much ma'am. And be quick now, I don't want to miss our boarding call. Why don't you go along too, Julie. Make sure to keep things quick and smooth, you hear?"

Samantha rose as she met Jackson's hardened eyes, and confirmed understanding with the affirmative nod of her head. Jackson kept his eyes fixed stone cold into the children's backs as they walked toward the bathroom, feeling slightly panicked that the girls would seize this unavoidable opportunity to out themselves and plea for help. He second-guessed himself for sending Samantha along, for she would be the one smart enough to understand their chance for escape. To not send her though, would be to risk the little one speaking out accidentally should the woman start asking her hard questions. He made the right choice he confirmed, holding to his hope that Samantha would indeed remain silent and scared with the alternative outcome he had promised for them.

"Go on in, now, and help out your little sister," said the woman once inside the bathroom as Daisy ran straight into the first open stall. "You girls okay?"

"What do you mean?" Asked Samantha, terrified Uncle Terry could somehow hear.

"Well, I don't know. Y'all seem a little nervous is all. Scared about such a long flight?" The woman asked.

"How long is it?" Samantha nervously replied.

"Bout 18 hours I'd say. Should be a real pretty view most of the way, though." She answered back.

Samantha flushed the toilet and helped Daisy pull up her pants, which now sagged down her little hips and tiny butt. "Do you have a phone?"

Samantha asked as she hoisted Daisy in her arms to reach into the water already running in the white porcelain sink.

"A phone?" The woman asked. "Can't say I do, left it in my bag when I checked in. Probably already in the belly of the bird as we speak. You sure you're okay, love?"

Samantha's heart sank as her hope vanished just as quickly as the thought popped into her head. She knew calling Brody wouldn't save them before they took off, anyway. But she had hoped to at least lead him in the right direction with the new information she had to offer. He could have done a lot with the names of their fake identity, and the flight number she had memorized as soon as they reached their designated gate.

"We're fine, I swear. Just nervous and excited for our vacation, ya know. We have never been in an airplane before," she said as she summoned a smile upon her face. "I wanted to call our mama one last time before we took off. Please don't tell our daddy, though. He will be mad that I tried to wake her cause she is really sick back at home and needs her rest."

"Your secret is safe with me," the woman confirmed as she pulled the bathroom door wide open and waited for the girls to walk through ahead. "Beautiful daughters, you have there. Simply delightful," said the sweet stranger to Jackson, as they all settled back into their proper seats.

"I am a lucky man," he replied with a pleasant tone, authenticity happy as relief rushed through his body and washed away the tension of the momentary separation from his prized property.

The woman nodded in agreement before returning her attention back to the romance novel, waiting face down on the chair next to her own. She would keep an eye on them all right, she thought to herself, as she picked up her book and pretended to read. And she was damn thankful to God for the long flight ahead, giving her enough time to figure out just what it was that bothered her so much. A woman whom spent a life in social work knew when children lied from years of practiced submissiveness and fear. Her trip to Thailand for the missionary service of its lost girls may not be her only reason for God's calling upon her, she realized, as her ears remained sharp in attention to the murmured interactions behind her seat.

A loud ding rang out to the waiting passengers, indicating boarding was underway. "Now boarding all small children and handicapped passengers," the flight attendant called through the microphone, the last checkpoint standing between Jackson and the success of his long-planned mission.

CHAPTER 44

Brody arrived to the airport and left his car running in the valet lane as he ran through the sliding automatic doors, which separated apart in a gliding swish of efficiency. He focused immediately on the schedule of departing flights, and memorized each one with the God-given skill of a photographic memory. He confirmed flight number 632 was still grounded with its departure time still intact, just ten minutes away. Just as he was about to deliberately disobey orders and run through the airport with his badge in hand, all flight departure times clicked into delayed status, one right after the other.

Brody sighed in relief, grateful for the infinite reach-of-power the FBI provided. He

walked back towards the doors as he phoned
Townsend for their estimated time-of-arrival,
only to be instead met by the Agents as they
marched through the sliding glass with full and
serious authority.

"Brody," Townsend greeted as he passed
by, sending Cooper and the Detective to follow
behind his lead. The men cut straight in front of
the waiting line as Townsend flashed his
identification to ward off any angry outbursts
from the impatient mob, already agitated and
ready to fight from the unexplained delay of their
respective flights. They headed to the first empty
station as the woman behind the desk looked at
them in confusion.

"Have you seen these people come
through here?" Said Townsend, as his partner laid
photo images of the girls and Jackson on top of
the counter.

"I think so," the woman responded.
"Pretty sure they checked in with Summer," she
said, as she pointed to the portly woman sitting
behind the counter, three stations away.

"Thank-you," said Brody, as the men
walked away.

"Sure," she said, as her anxious gaze met
Summer's questioning face.

"Can I help you gentlemen?" Summer asked, as Cooper displayed the images once more.

"Did you process these passengers, ma'am?" Asked Townsend, as she focused on the faces staring up from the counter below.

"Yes, sir. I sure did. They came through just 30 minutes ago, I'd say."

"And where are they headed?" Townsend replied.

"Bangkok, Thailand. Flight 632. What's going on? Does this have to do with the flight delays?" She asked.

But the men left her without response to stand shell-shocked behind, as they charged ahead toward their confirmed destination. "FBI," the Agents said as they held up their badge adorned hands and ran through every security checkpoint, gaining a trail of TSA personnel after each one they left behind. They reached the empty holding area as the boarded plane sat waiting for the go-ahead to resume its taxi toward the runway.

"What is this about?" Demanded the lead airport security official.

"Kidnapping," Brody said flatly.

"Get that plane back to the gate now," demanded Townsend in return, thoroughly dominating the officer's own authoritative questioning in an instant.

"Yes, sir," he responded, fully understanding the severity of the situation.

Just hold on Sam, thought Brody, as his eyes locked onto the colossal Boeing 747 sitting just outside the window. The security official went straight to the TSA Administrator, the top of the organization's chain-of-command, and the empty waiting room filled with fervent life once again. Brody could see the workers launch forward into action below as well, rolling the boarding tunnel back into place.

———————◆———————

Jackson's began to sweat, as the plane remained idle just off from the airport gate. Even though he kept reassuring himself that he had won, that this slight delay was not only normal, but also fully expected from the ignorance in charge of travel nowadays. But his pulse continued to rise in panic, and his deteriorating mind rested on the verge of sheer madness.

"How long do you think we will sit here?" Asked Samantha, just as a man's voice echoed through the speakers of the enclosed metal tube.

"This is your captain, here. We have just a slight delay. Hold tight and we will be ascending into this beautiful morning sky before you know it," the pilot reassured.

"Don't ask any questions," Jackson scolded Samantha in return. "Keep your mouth shut." He then grabbed the attention of a flight attendant as she passed by. "What is the hold up?" He asked in irritation.

"Just minor routine maintenance. And thank you for your continued patience, we will be off in no time," she answered. "Oh, and don't worry. I am sure the captain will make up for your lost time once in the air," she finished before walking toward the call light ahead.

The captain and copilot remained sealed behind the soundproof cockpit door as they received information regarding their ordered delay. They learned that the recent missing Michigan girls were not only still alive despite popular belief, but boarded with their capture upon their very own flight. The captain confirmed his orders from the control tower, drilled down from the FBI's command, and then carried his instructions out as he taxied the plane slowly forward.

When the plane finally began to move ahead, a cheer rang out from appreciative and eager passengers, while Jackson remained silent through his satisfied grin. Daisy looked out the window upon the mighty wing as the aircraft moved forward with life, and was overcome with subdued excitement. She hid her desire to squeal in delight from Uncle Terry, and concentrated hard to keep her excited legs stiff and still in her seat. Samantha smiled down to meet Daisy's eager face and hid her own sadness, as her daydream of rescue deflated around her heavy heart.

The excited chatter of surrounding passengers quickly faded away in confusion, as the plane turned in a complete circle at the ground stop and headed in reverse back toward the departing gate. "There is a slight change in plans," the captain explained through the speakers. "My copilot fell suddenly ill and cannot make the long trip ahead. We are hooking back up to exchange this sickly one next to me for a new and improved flying companion," he joked. "I apologize again for the delay, and I will have us in the air in no time at all."

And with the new announcement a shred of hope filled Sam's hollow heart once more, as Jackson's dangerous insanity plotted like a rabid animal, caged and cornered into a desperate mode of senseless attack.

"Please remain seated," a woman's voice called out from a pair of flight attendants as they walked toward the plane's sealed door. But

Jackson followed behind them through the long aisle ahead, and whispered his order into their stunned ears, as his lips hovered just between their parted heads.

"Don't touch that handle," he quietly demanded. "You march into that cockpit and tell that stupid son-of-a-bitch to get this plane in the air immediately."

"On whose authority?" Mocked the brunette, the shorter of the two.

"Mine," Jackson growled as he grabbed the sharp-tongued woman from behind and overtook her in an inescapable chokehold, growing instantly hard into her polyester skirt. The strength of the flight attendants fit and athletic muscles were no match against the power of Jackson's wild insanity.

"Oh my God!" A passenger screamed out, instantly alerting the attention of those nearby to witness the dangerous scene as it began to unfold.

"Everybody shut up!" Jackson screamed. Keep your mouths shut!" He demanded. "You," he pointed to the lanky blonde attendant who stood stiff with fear, her legs frozen in place. "Get this plane in the air before I snap her neck. "Now!" He screamed, which jolted her back with a sharp intake of breath, before she ran forward through her dizzied mind of disbelief.

Through the sudden commotion, the kind old woman slowly rose from her seat and walked five aisles forward before she sat in the empty seat Jackson had left behind. The girls looked at her through their dumbfounded eyes, confused by what they were supposed to do next. "I never properly introduced myself to you young-in's. My name is Ms. Mary. Let me help you."

"We don't need help, ma'am. But thank you anyway," Samantha replied through a most unconvincing voice.

"I know y'all are in trouble, angels. Do you need to get away from your daddy?" She asked.

Sam remained silent as the battle of speaking out in truth fought against their demanded role of fiction, not knowing which way paved the road with the guarantee of her sister's safety.

"You can trust me, love," Ms. Mary said to Samantha. "Let me help you, please. Your face tells me all I need to know." Just then, a shriek of many passengers blasted out in sudden unison and bounced off the walls of the aluminum confinement in a high-pitched echo, until the alarm of horror filled the ears of every single person aboard.

"Come with me," said Ms. Mary, as she led the girls from their seats and into the very back of the plane. She had just witnessed a helpless flight attendant fall to her death as soon as Jackson released her broken neck from his grasp, and she needed to get these two precious girls hidden away from the dangerous man ahead. "If he comes back this way, block his path," she said to each stunned passenger as she ushered the girls back. And they all felt a resolute responsibility to honor the woman's request, and nodded toward her in agreement. In fact, all of the men and women aboard became instantly connected in a single state of mind, a sudden united force of good against evil which consumed the mob with a righteous conviction to save not only the girls, but every life trapped aboard the imprisonment of one single, crazed man.

———————◆———————

The blonde flight attendant screamed in terror as her friend dropped dead to the ground as she returned toward them from the cockpit— with explicit instruction on how to handle the situation from the Captain. But her mind was now fully consumed with nothing more than the screaming demands of self-preservation, and she would instead follow the commands of the dark-haired killer alone.

"Took too long," Jackson explained, with an air of disregard for the vibrancy of life he had just brutally taken away. He laughed at the woman as tears streamed down her helpless face, unable to see the reality of his inevitable failure, as he soared above the weak and mindless through the potent high of his homicidal control. "I will say it again. Get your sweet little ass to the cockpit, and tell that coward hidden behind the door that I am the Captain now. I am in control. And he had better get this plane off the ground before I choose my next victim. And this time I won't choose so kindly," he laughed again, cackling through the broken mind of a maniac.

Again, the woman ran through the corridor in the vast strides offered by her long legs in complete obedience to the new man in charge. She past the air marshal on board whom remained camouflaged amongst the sea of hardened faces, all silently waiting to spring forward into action, all waiting for somebody else, however, to be the judge of when the timing was just right.

"Tick, Tick, Tick, who will be next?" Jackson mocked with pleasure, as he looked each passenger in the eye, pacing slowly back and forth. *Tick, Tick, Tick. Tock, Tock, Tock. Who will be the next victim of my clock?"* He sang out in

insanity. Jackson hadn't noticed when the window seat passengers had all followed suit, and, one by one, realized the brilliance of the first whom had quietly pulled down his blind to conceal the backward movement of the plane, and the Captain's direct refusal to adhere to Jackson's demand. And so, by the absence of any outside point-of-reference, and a mind lost inside the infatuation of complete power, Jackson did not notice the plane as it maneuvered into ready position next to the open gate, set up and ready to facilitate the rescuers which waited quietly inside.

The air marshal set his sights on the biggest passenger he could find, a burly linebacker type who looked bad-ass enough to charge straight into battle with the fearless adore that matched his own. He stared into the man's block-shaped face and hard set jaw and knew he was right, and that this man was about to charge from his seat at any moment. Once Jackson's back was turned as he continued his song of death in the opposite direction, the marshal tapped the leg of the adjacent passenger and pointed toward his targeted aid. And one by one, each passenger tapped attention to the other, until it reached the stiff body of strength, which sat in ready position at the edge of his seat. The man, his body thick with the bulk of pure muscle, led his gaze in the direction of the slight woman's outstretched and shaking finger beside him, and locked eyes with the marshal across the many hopeful faces in between, as he acknowledged and confirmed their newly formed partnership.

The Marshal pointed his finger toward the man, and then back to himself, signaling to the passenger that he was to act solely on the Marshal's lead, and not to move a second before he was given the order to do so. The stranger nodded again, in a gruff affirmation of his coach's instruction. As the flight attendant exited herself from the cockpit once more, she was stopped in front of the Air Marshal's outstretched arm, as he signaled with his head for her to stay put in the front of the plane.

Jackson's sing-song of madness came to an abrupt halt as his attention zoomed in on the empty seats of his property, of his slaves-in-waiting, and of his golden riches he so absolutely deserved. He roared out with furious rage, like a ravenous lion who'd lost against the weakness of its prey, and charged forward to rip his next victims apart with his bare hands and gnashing teeth. But at once, his path to the girls was blocked tightly shut, as each passenger stood shoulder to shoulder in a human shield of protection.

"Get outta my way!" Jackson screamed, as he clutched his hands around the neck of one unlucky man who stood steady in the front of the barricade, ready to fight with his own life to protect the lives of so many. But Jackson's sweaty grip was soon released as the force of attack overcame his strength, from both the men in front of the unwavering crowd, and from the sneak attack of the Marshal and his partner whom crept in from behind.

"Keep his hands behind his back!" Yelled the Marshal to his burly partner, as he slapped the hinged steel around Jackson's skinny wrists, and led him to the front of the plane as he applied threatening pressure into the back of Jackson's greasy black hair with the barrel of his government issued gun. "Open the passenger door," the Marshal instructed, as he held Jackson face down in the aisle, just in front of the now unsealed cockpit.

The shaken flight attendant released himself from the comforted embrace he held around his shock-stricken co-worker, and unsealed the plane's door with a vigorous and downward push upon the long handle. As soon as the door rose fully open, Brody rushed ahead and leapt over the space of tarmac below, as the plane sat slightly separated from the tunneled gate.

"Get him out of here," Brody bellowed out to the team of men, which followed behind. Jackson was pulled to his feet by his restrained arms as he thrashed wildly, ripping his own shoulder from its socket until it jutted out from his collarbone in a gnarly sight of twisted pain. Jackson became incoherent through his rabid screams of superiority, as the officers carried him through the airport, and into the waiting police cruiser as they recited his rights.

After securing the plane as close to the port as he could, the Captain and copilot joined Brody and the two FBI agents just as pandemonium began to erupt from the weary passengers. Their adrenaline subdued and a mournful anger set in. They witnessed the innocent woman, who had just a short time before greeted them all aboard with a youthfully bright smile, become sealed beneath the blackness of a body bag and wheeled away atop the white linen of the lifeless stretcher; leaving behind her loved ones, and her beloved career-in-the-clouds forever.

"The danger has been fully removed from the aircraft," Townsend called out through the Captain's speakers. "Remain seated and we will dismiss you in an orderly fashion." And again, Townsend's experienced voice full of command

and control had settled the rising tension in the air as the passenger's returned to their seats.

"Where are the girls?" Brody shouted, as he searched in every seat as he passed by.

"Back there," said a passenger as she pointed to the back of the plane.

Brody ran the length of the Boeing 747 with greedy impatience, which seemed to slow his legs in its murky mud before he reached the girls, still hidden in the small space behind the last row of seats, and guarded by a feisty old woman whom demanded to see his badge.

"Brody!" Samantha screamed as she leapt from her defensive fetal position behind the obscurity of the blue seats, past the firm frailty of Ms. Mary's hip, and straight into Brody's outstretched arms. He hugged her as she cried, and squeezed tighter and tighter as his own eyes welled with grateful relief.

"Ouch!" Samantha laughed, as her giddiness sent giggles from her soul to intertwine with the sobs of her rescued heart.

"I'm so sorry!" Brody laughed, as he released the stronghold of his embrace, reminding himself that Samantha would not slip through his protection and into danger, ever again.

Sam turned to get her baby girl, who was already out from hiding and wrapped around Ms. Mary's beige floral, ankle length skirt. "Daisy, come meet Detective Brody. He saved us, just like I knew he would," she said, as her sparkling eyes met his once again.

"Hello, Daisy," Brody replied, as he stuck out his hand with respect to the unsure little girl. She met her tiny hand in his as Samantha hugged her from behind. "I have heard so much about you, and here you are! I am so very excited to finally meet you," Brody continued.

"Nice to meet you, too," said Daisy, just above a timid whisper, as a smile crept wide across her face. And then, even young as she was, her intuition of authentic safety settled in and sent her running into Brody's arms. Samantha followed behind to join her sister and Brody, who had knelt upon his knees to reciprocate Daisy's hug on her own level. Agent Cooper made his way back just in time to see the three united into one, a mesh of little arms wrapped beneath the security of brute strength. The embrace seemed to pulse with a life of its own, generated from genuine love. He quickly captured the moment with the camera in his phone, knowing this memory would serve each of them with happiness for the rest of their lives.

Cooper cleared his throat. "Time to get going. We have an ambulance waiting just outside."

But Samantha remained gripped into Brody's warmth, with Daisy still squished heavenly in between, and refused to move from the security of her rescuer. Townsend joined the group to reunite with his team, and to share in the success of their happy ending. He lowered himself to the huddled trio as his knees cracked in frustrated opposition, and pulled Daisy's cheerful doll from his jacket. Daisy recognized the orange yarn against the black fabric of serious authority, and accepted the gesture of peace and comfort as she squeezed her baby tight into her newfound safety.

"Come on, girls," Brody said. "I won't leave you alone. I'll ride with you the whole way to the hospital and stay as long as you want me there, okay?"

"Promise?" Samantha asked.

"With my entire heart," Brody replied.

CHAPTER 45

Samantha sat next to Daisy's hospital bed which was adorned with bright Sesame Street sheets featuring Elmo, Big Bird, and the whole cheery gang. Even Oscar the Grouch seemed happy in his smelly trash can with the hopefulness that filled the little room. Daisy had been admitted for observation and treatment due to her injuries and malnutrition. Samantha, however, was thoroughly checked, cleared, and discharged once her cracked cast was removed and her fractured arm was set back in place under fresh plaster.

Rain pounded generously against the brick and glass of the third floor pediatric unit. Sam would not peel her eyes from Daisy as she fell into a peaceful slumber, with freshly washed hair and purified skin which now glowed as pink as a wild rose mallow. And as a fat raindrop succumbed to the pull of gravity and rolled slowly down the window at Sam's back, so, too, did a single tear fall in ultimate release, freed from pain as it traveled the path down Samantha's tender cheek, landing upon the top of Daisy's hand.

Brody kept his word and remained stationed in an extra sleep chair that a kind and understanding nurse had provided. After the nightmarish ordeal the children had been through, not one single person on the hospital staff would deny the girls any form of comfort, big or small, whether it broke their rigid protocol or not. The only time Brody left the room was to call Carly Chandler the minute Daisy was settled into her room. And even then, he remained just outside the door and in complete view during the entire conversation for the girls' reassurance. Brody's pulse pounded with the ferocity of love, and fought with valor against the will of his logic-driven mind the very moment Carly's voice filled his ears. But that feeling became a week shadow, like the dimming of a candle burned to the end of its wick, compared to his overwhelming need for Carly as she walked into the room. Her smile and scent, of both purity and sensuality combined, took control over the last of Brody's willful intentions. In that moment he let go of all the trepidation that, for years, had ruled his heart, and knew that his soul would forever yearn for the love of Carly for the rest of his dutiful life.

"Ms. Chandler!" Sam cried out, as the two met in each other's arms in the middle of the room.

"My sweet Samantha," Carly returned, as she held her at arms length to see that Sam was indeed safe and unharmed. "I am so sorry, babe. So sorry. I should have kept you by my side," Carly cried out as she embraced her once more.

"No, no. It's my fault. Please don't say you're sorry, not after all you've done for me. And I'm not sorry, anyway. Not at all. It needed to happen this way. I would have never gotten my Daisy back if I didn't go with him. I would've never seen her again," Sam said with the advanced wisdom of a survivor's past. "I would do it again, and then again," she continued, "and I will keep her safe for the rest of my life."

"What a lucky girl she is," Carly confirmed. "She is blessed, you both are, to have each other to love for the rest of your lives. I don't know where I would be, even as happy as I am now, if I had the strength of a sister like you."

"You are perfect," Samantha countered. "Beautiful and perfect."

Daisy stirred from the sudden activity in the room, and Sam went straight to her side as her little angel sat up and smiled toward them from her bed. "I have to go potty," she said as she kicked her legs free from beneath the sheets. Samantha walked with her, hand in hand, while she gingerly maneuvered Daisy's IV stand along and into the bathroom labeled 'for patient use only'.

As soon as the bathroom door clicked shut, Brody rose to his feet and stepped toward Carly with slow and hungry strides. Carly fought to catch her breath and steady her trembling body as she locked eyes with the man she now loved. He walked toward her without hesitation, without fear, and without apology for his transparent intentions. As their bodies crashed into one another, the greed of lust and love burned from the center of their beating hearts to the surface of their skin, encircling them with the consuming fire of need. Carly fell weak into Brody's embrace, as he possessed her mouth with his lips, unlocking once more the fragile trust of her yearning heart. Only this time, there was no going back. No way to reseal the passion which now flowed through her blood, the kind of passion she thought was impossible, thought was irreversibly stolen from her long ago. Brody would now and forever hold the key, which unlocked her world and cultivated her spirit to the highest level of joy. She wanted to float in this alternate reality with Brody by her side, for the rest of her blessed life.

The flush of the toilet, loud with its industrial strength pressure, echoed in the room as it forcefully hiccupped the last of the water down its porcelain drain. Carly and Brody released from the intimate exchange, which told them more than their words could have expressed, and jumped back from one another from fear of being caught. Neither wanted to scare or confuse the girls with questions right now, it was the very last thing their minds needed. Little did either of them know, that Samantha had already begun to daydream about living out the life of her fantasies with Carly and Brody by her side, with the kind of parents they would be, and with the love they could provide for her Daisy to grow and blossom from beneath rich and healthy soil.

CHAPTER 46

A few weeks had passed and both Carly and Brody had taken time off work; Brody a full month, and Carly the rest of the school year. The case the DA had presented against Arlene and Jackson was so concrete, they both pled guilty under the advisement of their appointed attorneys, and a received a sentence, without the possibility of parole, for the remainder of their natural lives. And even though the girls were now forever safe from a life of torture and abuse, Brody and Carly were both selfishly grateful that Samantha held the Detective to his promise, and requested he stay in the large Chandler home every day and night since Daisy's hospital release.

"I have to keep my word to stay by their side," Brody would say.

"Of course, you do. They need you just as deeply as they need me," Carly would always agree.

Todd set up camp with his parents, and offered the Detective his room for as long as need be. He, too, was selfishly grateful. And optimistic his Carly would get the real happy ending she deserved, as he could see the hopeless love and admiration seeping from their eyes on the very day they brought the girls home.

"Girls all settled?" Brody asked, as Carly joined him in front of the fire.

"Sleeping beneath the prayers of the angels," she said. "And snoring like a pair of old men, too."

Brody chuckled, as he scooped Carly into the nook beneath his strong arm, with the statuesque curves of his tanned muscles fully exposed under the white cotton of his undershirt. His warmth drove Carly mad with desire, as she stroked the skin of his defined chest with her fingertips. Brody cuddled his face into the curve of her neck, as her soft touch sent him into longing right along with her. "I have a question," he said, as he playfully nipped into the flesh just below her ear.

"What is it?" She groaned, and played along as she guided her hand down from his chest to explore the delight of his abs below.

"How did you afford all of this on a teacher's salary?" He asked, as he emphasized the 'all of this' part with wave of his hand across the spacious room.

"That, was NOT the question I was expecting," Carly laughed, as she sat up and detangled herself from his grasp, forced to tickle under his arm when he would not let her go. "Funny thing, karma is. Or the universe, or God's will, whatever you call it. Turns out my mother's mother, my grandma that I had never met, was quite well off. Loaded, actually. Like, old-money, oil type rich. She was on her deathbed when my mother was arrested for my abuse. The police found her when searching for any next-of-kin to place me with, before they gave custodial rights to Todd's parents. My mother and her had some sort of falling out; I'll never know what it was exactly about. Anyway, my grandmother had been searching for her for years with hope, from what she told the police officer, that she had sobered up and changed her ways."

"Go on," said Brody, as he slid his body to hold her against his chest once more.

"Yeah. So, long story short, once she found out what my mother had done, and the details of my abuse from the court reports, she changed her will. Cut my mother out, and left everything to me. Her husband had passed years before, and I was the only blood relative she had left. She died just a day after her lawyer had come to her house and prepared her final wishes. She passed before I could meet her, before I knew of the trust fund she had set up in my name, and before I could thank her for the beautiful letter she left behind for me. But somehow I feel her, feel her connection, and I know through her kind words that I came from the solid roots of good and loving people. Despite how much my own mother hated me, and hated me even more with each breath I took."

"I love you," Brody said suddenly. "And with every breath you take, I will love you even more."

"I love you, too," Carly said through her silent tears. I loved you the moment I saw you, I think. And I loved you fully once you brought those sweet girls back home to me. I am never letting them go, you know," she said as she pointed toward the hallway above, and to the room where her children slept in each other's arms.

"I know that. I love you for that. And I'm never letting you go, either. Not you, or our precious girls. My heart will beat with the love for the three of you until the day I die."

"My Teddy," Carly whispered, before giving her equal and endless devotion with the sacred gift she had never, and would never, give to another man. They made love in front of the soft orange glow of a slow burning fire, and then laid in each others arms as they whispered their promises of devotion and eternity until the early morning hours. They smiled while locked into each others gaze, just as the house filled with sun's warm light and the coo of a mourning dove's song; calling out its own beautiful promise of loyalty in the distance, high atop a mighty birch tree.

THE END

Note from the Author

I BELIEVE WE MUST SEEK OUR PURPOSE, BELIEVE IN OUR TALENTS, AND HONOR OUR DREAMS—AND ENCOURAGE OTHERS TO DO THE SAME. THROUGH THIS I HAVE DISCOVERED SELF-WORTH AND TRUE HAPPINESS. AIM TO INSPIRE AND ACT WITH KINDNESS, ALWAYS.

"KEEP AWAY FROM PEOPLE WHO TRY TO BELITTLE YOUR AMBITIONS. SMALL PEOPLE ALWAYS DO THAT, BUT THE REALLY GREAT MAKE YOU FEEL THAT YOU, TOO, CAN BECOME GREAT." ~ MARK TWAIN

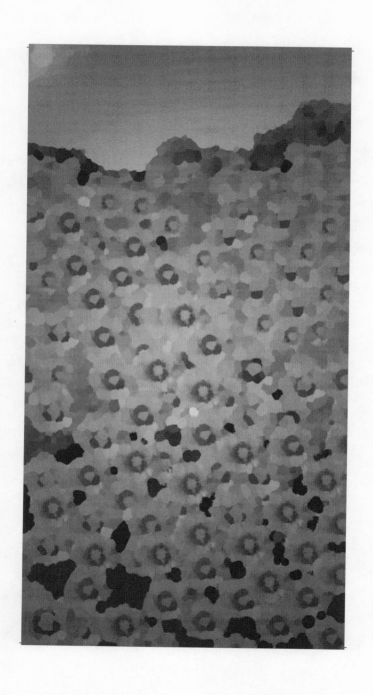

29365187R10215

Made in the USA
Charleston, SC
12 May 2014